Copyright Page

How to Register a Cat in Another Dimension
© 2025 by Silas Blackwood
All rights reserved.
No part of this book may be reproduced, stored, or transmitted in any form or by any means—electronic, mechanical, photocopying, recording, or otherwise—without written permission from the author, except in the case of brief quotations used in reviews or critical articles.

This is a work of fiction. Any resemblance to actual persons, cats (legal or illegal), or interdimensional government agencies is purely coincidental. Probably.

First edition, 2025

To every cat who registered their human
long before their human ever noticed.
And to the toast that never stood a chance.

"Some people adopt cats.
Some cats adopt people.

And some cats file paperwork about it."

— Bureau of Interdimensional Emotional Companionship, Article 3B

CONTENT

FOREWORD 5

CHAPTER ONE: THE CAT WHO SHOWED UP WITHOUT PAPERS . 7

CHAPTER TWO: THE BUREAU AND THE TABBY 31

CHAPTER THREE: THREE LETTERS AND A FORMAL AFFAIR 80

CHAPTER FOUR: THE ART OF STANDING STILL 126

CHAPTER FIVE: THE CLAREMONT ECHO 187

CHAPTER SIX: THE COUNCIL OF COMPLAINTS 256

CHAPTER SEVEN: THE CAT, THE CODE, AND THE COUNCIL TAX 314

CHAPTER EIGHT: TWO CATS, ONE TOAST CRISIS 354

AUTHOR'S NOTE 402

A NOTE TO KEKE 403

Foreword

There are two types of people in this world:

those who live with cats,

and those who think they're the ones in charge.

This book is for both.

When I first started writing How to Register a Cat in Another Dimension, I thought it would be a short, silly thing.

Something with whiskers, toast, and probably an unnecessary number of magical forms.

But somewhere between Grace's existential admin crisis and Leo's smug naps, I realised I wasn't writing about cats at all.

I was writing about what happens when we try—awkwardly, slowly, beautifully—to let something (or someone) matter to us again.

Even when the paperwork says we shouldn't.

This story came out of long walks with no answers, mugs of tea gone cold beside unread forms, and a small orange cat who showed up at the worst and best possible time.

It's for anyone who's ever resisted connection... and ended up filing an emotional registration anyway.

So, if you're holding this book: welcome.

You're officially part of the Claremont System now.

Your toast consumption may be monitored.

Your emotional barriers may be gently challenged.

Your cat may be reading over your shoulder.

I hope you enjoy the chaos, the warmth, and the paperwork.

And I hope—when the moment comes—you, too, choose to stay.

— Silas, B 2025

Chapter One: The Cat Who Showed Up Without Papers

Part 1

Arrival by Ironing Board and Bureaucratic Threat

If there was one thing Grace Harper was absolutely sure of, it was that cats should not fall out of shimmering portals directly onto your ironing board.

Yet here she was, holding a half-melted steam iron and staring at a large, indignant tabby who had apparently chosen her London flat as his point of arrival into... well, whatever cosmic nonsense this was.

The cat blinked at her. Slowly. Judgmentally. As if *she* were the one trespassing in *his* kitchen.

It wasn't the weirdest thing that had happened to Grace this month. But it definitely made the Top Five.

"Right," she said aloud. "Of course. Why not. Tuesday's perfect for interdimensional cat delivery."

The cat meowed.

It sounded smug.

* * *

Grace had always considered herself a practical person. She worked in IT support, wore socks that matched, and hadn't screamed once during the great blender explosion of 2022.

But even practical people have limits.

Especially when the newly-arrived tabby casually hopped onto the counter, opened a drawer with one paw, and pulled out her emergency packet of tuna.

"I— How did you know where that was?!"

The cat made a sound halfway between a chirp and a cough.

Then coughed again.

Then, with zero warning, **spoke**.

"I'm not here to answer questions," it said, in a voice that sounded like Benedict Cumberbatch doing an impression of a tax auditor. "I'm here for your signature."

Grace dropped the tuna.

* * *

The next hour was... bureaucratically traumatic.

The cat — who introduced himself, unironically, as **Leo** — explained that in his dimension, cats were considered dual-citizen magical beings called *Feliform Sentients*, and required registration under something called the **Cross-Plane Feline Coexistence Act**.

Which would've been fine.

Except Leo didn't have his paperwork.

And because he arrived on Grace's property — more specifically, on her ironing board — she was now legally classified as his **Sponsor of Record**.

"Hold on," Grace said. "You're telling me that because you crashed into *my* kitchen without so much as a meow of warning, I'm now your... guardian?"

"Technically," Leo sniffed, licking his paw, "you're my Legal Interface Anchor. It's a temporary designation."

"Temporary like jury duty, or temporary like herpes?"

Leo blinked slowly. "That depends how well you fill out forms."

* * *

It turned out that "registering a cat from another dimension" involved a staggering amount of paperwork, some of which was in cursive, and all of which had to be signed with **ink derived from metaphorical intent**.

Grace stared at the first form, titled:

Form 3-B: Declaration of Cross-Species Sentient Companion Acquisition

There was a note scribbled in the corner that read:
"DO NOT FORGE. MAGICAL CONSEQUENCES MAY APPLY. Also, keep the cat fed."

"I am not," she muttered, "qualified for this."

But Leo was already curled on her sofa, purring like he'd paid rent.

*　*　*

Interlude: The Orange Cat's Journal (Entry #01)

Name: Leo
Species: Feliform Sentient (Variant: Bureau-Certified Tabby)
Mission: Secure anchor point in human dimension.
Status: Arrived. Landed on ironing board. Acquired tuna.
Human Assessment:
– Hair: Slightly chaotic
– Eyes: Expressive, occasionally panicked
– Paperwork skills: Unproven
– Potential for Chaos: Moderate-to-concerning

Recommend observation. May require snacks to maintain cooperation.

Part 2

Inspectors, Neighbours, and Interdimensional Judgement

By Wednesday, Grace had:

1. Missed two work meetings,
2. Learned the difference between a "Feliform Sentient" and a "Plain Cat," and
3. Accidentally opened a magical hotline by microwaving a silver spoon with Leo's pawprint on it.

The hotline operator had sounded disturbingly cheerful.

"Thank you for contacting the Bureau of Interplanar Cross-Species Affairs! For cat registration, press 1. For fox registration, press 2. For ferret emergencies, scream."

Grace had pressed 1.

Then immediately regretted it.

* * *

"YOU DON'T HAVE A FORM 7-E?"

The Bureau voice had dropped three octaves.

"No, I wasn't *issued* a Form 7-E," Grace replied, clutching the phone. "You see, the cat—Leo—arrived unannounced, through a magical portal that incinerated my tea towels. I didn't get a welcome pack."

There was a pause.

Then:

"Are you currently in possession of a metaphysically unlicensed feline entity?"

Grace looked at Leo, who was lounging across three couch cushions like a feline monarch.

"...Technically?"

"That's a yes. We're dispatching someone."

She hung up.

Leo blinked at her.

"Excellent," he said. "They'll bring the paperwork."

Grace glared. "You could've mentioned they also send *inspectors*."

"Oh yes," Leo said smugly. "But then you might've tried to run."

* * *

The inspector arrived at 4:17 p.m., precisely.

She was short, wore aggressively pointy shoes, and carried a clipboard that levitated behind her like a judgmental drone.

Her name was **Mrs. Penumbra**, and she smelled faintly of sage and legal threats.

"You've been reported for unlicensed cross-realm sponsorship," she said. "Where's the cat?"

Leo strutted in from the kitchen, holding a cracker in his mouth.

"Charmed," he said around crumbs.

Mrs. Penumbra stared at him.

Then stared at Grace.

"I see," she muttered. "One of *those* cases."

Grace wasn't sure what *those* meant, but she didn't like the sound of it.

* * *

It got worse.

The inspector pulled out a form labelled TCS-419-B: "Neighbourhood Notification of Magical Entities (Feline Class, Class B+ or Above)" and handed it to Grace.

"You are legally required to notify all neighbouring residences within 100 feet of any magical feline presence," she said. "Failure to do so within 72 hours results in a citation and automatic registration into the Neighbourhood Watch Review Committee."

Grace blinked. "Neighbourhood what?"

Penumbra snapped her fingers.

The clipboard handed Grace a scroll.

Leo looked over her shoulder and winced.

"Oh," he said. "That's the committee with the nosy pensioners and the old tabby who runs surveillance on Tuesdays."

"You mean Mr. Clovis?" Grace asked. "The grumpy ginger cat next door?"

"He's not grumpy," Leo muttered. "He's ex-Bureau."

*　*　*

By Thursday morning, Grace's doorbell rang no fewer than nine times.

- Mrs. Hargrove from flat 2B brought lemon biscuits and two pages of passive-aggressive notes about "cat dander aura disruption".
- A ginger tabby sat on her welcome mat for forty-five minutes, meowing in Morse code.

- And someone anonymously slid this note under her door:

"We see you. We know that is not a registered British cat. You'll be hearing from us."
— The Neighbourhood Watch (Magical Division)

Grace screamed into her couch pillow.

Leo sat beside her, purring comfortably.

"See?" he said. "We're already becoming part of the community."

She muffled a scream.

* * *

Interlude: The Orange Cat's Journal (Entry #02)

Inspection Outcome:
– Bureau status: Complicated
– Human's tolerance: Holding steady
– Surveillance risk: Elevated (see Clovis)

Neighbourhood assessment:
– 12% friendly
– 63% nosy
– 25% possibly magical retirees with unclear allegiances

Action Items:
– Acquire Form 7-E

– Locate "Lady Tabby of Flat 4D" (rumoured to control biscuit distribution)
– Prevent Grace from combusting emotionally

Snack Index:
– Tuna: Available
– Crackers: Acceptable
– Cursed sardines from dimension 4H: DO NOT REPEAT

* * *

Part 3

Dry Cleaners, Forms, and Bureaucratic Bonding

By Friday morning, Grace had fully accepted the following facts:

1. Her cat was not a cat.
2. Her neighbours were possibly part of a magical surveillance state.
3. And she, Grace Harper — IT support technician and part-time plant whisperer — was now legally responsible for a smug, paperwork-deficient interdimensional feline bureaucrat in loaf form.

Naturally, the only logical response was **caffeine**.

Unfortunately, her local café was now **off-limits**, thanks to Leo's "little incident" involving a self-stirring espresso and a barista named Fiona who may or may not have been half-goblin.

"Look," Leo said as they walked down the street, "she started it."

"She *asked* if you wanted whipped cream," Grace replied. "That's not a declaration of war."

"She said it like it was *optional*," Leo sniffed. "And my dignity is not optional."

* * *

Their destination was **The Bureau of Interplanar Licensing and Arcane Taxation (Local Branch 7B)** — which was, confusingly, housed in the back room of a dry cleaner called *Press to Impress*.

The front smelled like detergent and broken dreams.

The back smelled like bureaucracy and faintly lemon-scented dread.

A glowing sign over the counter read:

NOW SERVING: C-18
CURRENT WAIT TIME: 2-4 weeks

Grace sighed.

Leo, naturally, leapt onto the counter and curled into a ball.

"I nap, you queue," he said, yawning. "We all serve in our own way."

Grace glared at him. "You're the *reason* we're here."

"Yes, and you're the anchor. This is a team sport."

* * *

Two hours later, she was seated across from a Bureau clerk with aggressively blue lipstick, seven pens levitating above her desk, and a nameplate that read **"Verity (she/her/they/the Witness)"**.

Verity did not blink often. Or at all.

"You're attempting to register a spontaneous cross-dimensional Companion," Verity said flatly.

"Yes."

"Without a pre-filed Feline Intent Manifestation Certificate."

Grace nodded slowly.

"And with no digital trace of pre-existing bond indicators, signature alignment, or memory blending."

"That sounds correct," Grace replied.

Verity sighed. The pens drooped slightly.

"Do you at least have Form 7-E?"

Grace pulled out the form she'd been handed by Penumbra. It was sticky, partially crumpled, and possibly had pawprints in marmalade.

Verity stared at it.

Then stared at Grace.

"...Did your cat eat jam?"

Leo looked up from the counter. "It was *apricot chutney*. Don't be gauche."

* * *

Verity handed her a new scroll.

"Take this to Office 3C," they said. "Ask for Timothy. He handles cases involving accidental bonds between civilians and *non-compliant magical feliforms*."

Grace stood. "That's oddly specific."

"We're hiring someone for just parrots next month," Verity said dryly. "It's a growing market."

* * *

Office 3C was guarded by a magical security seal that demanded a **riddle**.

Grace stared at it for ten seconds.

"WHAT COMES BEFORE CAT?" the door boomed.

"...Uh, what?"

"WHAT COMES BEFORE CAT?"

Leo raised a paw lazily. "That's just a bureaucratic joke. The answer's 'form'."

Grace said it aloud.

The door unlocked with a *sad little meow* and swung open.

Inside was a man with three ties, two clipboards, and what looked suspiciously like a small jellyfish floating in a coffee cup.

"Grace Harper?" he said.

She nodded.

"Please state the nature of your bond with the accused feline."

"...Accused?!"

"It's just a formality."

Grace took a deep breath.

"We met when he crashed into my kitchen via a portal. He ate my tuna. He talked. And now he sleeps in my laundry basket."

Timothy blinked.

"That counts. Continue."

* * *

The next forty minutes involved:

- One magical identity scan (Leo's tail interfered),
- Three argument forms (Classified as: 'Feline Belligerence – Mild to Smug'),
- And a **mandatory visual bond confirmation ritual**, which was essentially Leo sitting in Grace's lap while a Bureau orb whispered, "Consent confirmed" and blew confetti.

Grace sneezed glitter for ten straight minutes.

Timothy handed her the official interim license scroll.

"Congratulations," he said. "You're now an *Uncertified Feliform Companion Liaison, Grade Q*. That gives you 30 days to complete full integration paperwork and avoid cross-species housing violations."

Grace stared at the scroll.

"...I'm sorry, 'Grade Q'?"

"It stands for 'Questionable but Legal.'"

* * *

Back outside the Bureau building, Leo stretched, yawned, and casually batted a pigeon off the bench.

"Well," he said, "that went better than expected."

"I have to take a six-part online ethics course now," Grace said, reading the fine print.

"Better than cross-dimensional community service. Trust me."

Grace squinted at him. "Have you done that?"

Leo looked away. "No comment."

* * *

Interlude: The Orange Cat's Journal (Entry #03)

Human Status:
– Emotionally frayed
– Legally entangled
– Morally still superior

Mission Progress:
– Acquired interim license
– Avoided full magical audit
– Confirmed bond with impressive lap compatibility

Threats:
– Bureau curiosity (mild)
– Clovis surveillance (elevated)
– Grace reading the fine print (ongoing risk)

Snack Forecast:

– Milk: Promising

– Scones: Negotiable

– Jellyfish in Bureau mug: Declined

* * *

Part 4

Three Letters and the Ginger Tribunal

Saturday morning arrived with the grim certainty of unpaid rent and overripe bananas.

Grace had barely recovered from her Bureau adventure when a scroll materialised above her kettle, hovered for a moment, and smacked her in the face.

She peeled it off, unfolded it, and read the heading:

SUPPLEMENTAL LICENSE REQUIREMENTS – URGENT

As per Regulation 5.3(c), all temporary Feline Companion Liaisons (Grade Q) must submit a **Three-Recommendation Letter Pack** within seven business days.

At least one letter must be from:

1. A current or former Companion with verified magical presence;
2. A non-familial local human resident with no criminal record;
3. A magically literate neighbour, civic official, or registered cross-dimensional witness.

Failure to comply may result in fine, demotion to Grade R (Rogue Potential), or magical probation.

Grace groaned.

Leo, currently perched on the windowsill watching pigeons commit air crimes, didn't even blink.

"I need three letters," she said. "From three different people. Or magical beings. Or some combination of the above."

Leo finally turned. "You mean my fan club."

"More like your probation committee."

"Details."

* * *

1. The Companion Reference — Mr Clovis, Retired Bureau Agent, Feline (Ginger)

Grace started with the worst option first.

Clovis, the cranky orange tabby from two floors down, had previously expressed his opinion of Leo by hissing and peeing on a flowerpot.

Grace brought tuna. Fancy tuna.

Clovis sat on his cushion like a Victorian landlord, tail twitching in quiet judgment.

"You wish me to vouch for *him*," Clovis said, voice gravelly and with an accent that could only be described as 'Colonial Disappointment'.

"He's... unorthodox," Grace admitted.

"He once tried to unionise the mice."

Grace blinked. "He what?"

Clovis sighed. "I was Bureau once. I've seen worse. At least he's not one of those *quantum panthers*."

He scratched behind his ear thoughtfully.

"I'll write the letter. But only because the last time I refused a request, someone turned into a cactus."

Grace chose not to ask.

* * *

2. The Local Human Resident — Mrs. Netherby, Flat 4D, Widow, Gossip Engine

Mrs. Netherby was 80% floral wallpaper, 15% cinnamon biscuits, and 5% passive aggression.

She answered the door in full housecoat regalia and a pearl necklace that looked magical *but wasn't* — she just wore it for drama.

"You're the one with the talking cat," she said, squinting.

Grace smiled. "He prefers 'verbally expressive.'"

"He knocked over my azaleas."

"He's... enthusiastic."

Mrs. Netherby nodded slowly, then stepped aside. Her flat smelled like a cross between lavender tea and very old scandal.

"I'll write the letter," she said. "On one condition."

Grace waited.

"I want visitation rights."

"Visitation—?"

"I like cats that talk back. You can't yell at normal cats without feeling silly."

"...Deal."

* * *

3. The Magically Literate Neighbour — Trevor from 3B, Conspiracy Theorist / Rune Hobbyist

Trevor answered the door wearing a tinfoil hat and a hoodie that said *"WIZARDS ARE REAL. I WORK IN HR."*

He looked at Grace, then looked past her.

"Is the orange one with you?"

Leo padded into view.

Trevor gasped. "OH MY GOD, HE'S A FLUX ANIMAL!"

Grace had no idea what that meant.

Leo meowed with dramatic flair.

Trevor nearly cried. "He SPOKE to me. I've waited my whole life for this."

Grace handed him the scroll template. "You just need to write a short endorsement—"

Trevor vanished into his flat, emerged 47 seconds later with a letter written in glitter ink on rune-embossed stationery that smelled faintly of nutmeg.

TO WHOM IT MAY CONCERN:
The orange one is my spiritual mentor and may be a reincarnated phoenix.
Please grant him ALL THE PASSES.
I would follow him into battle.
Yours in reverence,
Trevor
(Knight of the Third Laundry Room Circle)

Leo purred approvingly.

* * *

By late afternoon, Grace had three letters, one cup of rapidly cooling tea, and a headache shaped like a bureaucratic badger.

She stared at the scrolls laid out before her.

"I can't believe this is real," she muttered.

Leo leapt onto the table.

"Reality is just consensus plus paperwork," he said. "Congratulations. You're halfway to legitimacy."

She glared. "I don't *want* legitimacy. I want my normal life back."

Leo gave her a long look.

"Too late," he said.

Then, more gently: "But maybe that's not so bad."

Grace didn't reply.

But she didn't throw the letters out, either.

* * *

Interlude: The Orange Cat's Journal (Entry #04)

Human Progress:
— Acquired all three required letters
— Did not faint, scream, or hex anyone (impressive restraint)

Social Integration Notes:
— Clovis: Grumpy, but bribable
— Mrs. Netherby: Dangerous in the way only grandmothers can be
— Trevor: Fanboy, must not be given actual spells

Emotional Analysis:
— Human is adapting faster than expected
— Possible bond strengthening
— Potential for future chaos: Extremely promising

Next Objective:
— Submit letters

– Survive Bureau's Verification Gala
– Avoid wearing a tie

Chapter Two: The Bureau and the Tabby

Part 1

Grace had never been to a magical government building before, but she was fairly certain they weren't supposed to smell like damp socks and ambition.

She stood in front of **The Bureau of Interplanar Licensing and Arcane Taxation (West London Sub-Branch)** — tucked inside what used to be a discount mattress store — clutching a file folder labelled in blocky biro:

"Leo's Stuff (Probably Important)."

Leo, in contrast, had arrived via mailbox.

She still wasn't sure how.

* * *

He popped out with all the elegance of a smug spring-loaded loaf and landed on the pavement beside her, stretching luxuriously.

"This is your big day," he purred. "Try not to embarrass us."

Grace rolled her eyes. "You're not even wearing a collar."

Leo sniffed. "Because I'm not livestock."

"You're not paperwork-compliant either."

"Neither are most politicians, and look how well they do."

* * *

The Bureau's reception hall looked like someone had tried to blend Hogwarts with a tax office and failed spectacularly at both.

On the left wall:

- A bulletin board with titles like:
    - "New Protocols for Portal Etiquette (Don't Fall Out Screaming)"
    - "Reminder: Do NOT Feed the Mailboxes"

On the right wall:

- A vending machine that dispensed **emotionally infused tea** (Chamomile of Acceptance was sold out), and something called *"Regret Latte."*

And straight ahead — a glowing reception desk guarded by an older woman with an aggressively floral brooch and the kind of expression that suggested she had personally survived seven bureaucratic wars and enjoyed none of them.

"Name?" she barked.

Grace stepped forward. "Grace Harper. I'm here to submit a companion bond registration — Form 7-E with attachments."

The receptionist looked over her glasses. "With that cat?"

Leo waved a paw.

The woman sighed deeply and rang a desk bell that let out a sharp yelp.

A floating clipboard appeared with a WHUMP.

* * *

After signing six scrolls, two glowing orbs, and a biscuit (don't ask), Grace was handed a slim ticket with a number on it:

"Now Serving: G-402"

Her number was G-847.

Leo hopped onto the waiting bench beside her and began grooming his tail like he was at a spa.

Grace slumped beside him.

"Remind me again why this matters?"

"Because if I don't get licensed," Leo said between licks, "you'll be fined, I'll be deported, and Trevor will probably start a 'Free the Tabby' protest outside your flat."

Grace groaned.

"I just wanted a normal life."

Leo yawned. "Then you shouldn't have lived near a dimensional rift. Or owned tuna."

* * *

Two hours and a stale muffin later, a glowing orb floated by and barked her name — literally. "Harper. Grace. Room 3A. Move it."

Leo stretched and leapt to the floor. "Showtime."

Room 3A looked like a cross between a Victorian study and a sentient filing cabinet.

The air shimmered slightly.

At the far end sat a woman in an eggplant-coloured blazer, surrounded by floating typewriters and what appeared to be a talking fern muttering legal jargon.

"Grace Harper," the woman said. "I'm Auditor Shard. Welcome to the Companion Licensing Preliminary Verification Suite."

Grace opened her mouth.

Leo beat her to it. "We brought snacks."

* * *

Auditor Shard raised one eyebrow.

Leo continued smoothly. "Grace is my assigned anchor. I am a Level-3 sentient with Bureau-affiliated history, and I come bearing three recommendation letters—"

"You were unlicensed."

Leo's tail twitched.

"You were caught without dimensional tags."

"That was a clerical error. I fell through the wrong portal."

"You landed on an ironing board."

"It was freshly padded."

Shard exhaled slowly. "Fine. Let's see the letters."

Grace handed them over, still unsure why the biscuit had required her signature earlier.

The Auditor scanned each scroll. Her face remained neutral until she reached Trevor's.

"'I would follow him into battle'?" she read aloud.

Grace smiled weakly. "He's... very enthusiastic."

Shard set the scrolls down.

"On paper, you pass. However—"

Leo immediately flattened his ears.

"—paper isn't everything. You'll need to complete a **Compatibility Audit**."

* * *

Grace blinked. "A what?"

Shard smiled for the first time. It was not comforting.

"Think of it as... magical couples therapy for humans and their sentient companions. Just to confirm you're not hiding any extradimensional parasites or engaging in illicit spirit hosting."

Leo blinked. "This feels discriminatory."

Shard slid a contract across the desk.

"It's mandatory."

Grace picked it up. The title read:

"Form 8-K: Emotional Coexistence Audit & Empathic Bond Integrity Assessment"

Underneath, in smaller text:
"Side effects may include magical fatigue, sudden clarity, and minor spiritual entanglement. Do not operate heavy machinery afterwards."

"Do I have a choice?" Grace asked.

"No," said Shard.

"Yes," said Leo.

"No," said the desk fern.

* * *

Part 2

The Compatibility Audit

The audit room looked like a yoga studio had eaten a therapy office and then gotten indigestion.

There were plush beanbags, softly glowing ambient lights, and a waterfall that burbled judgmentally in the corner. Grace immediately hated it.

"This feels like a spa run by introverts," she muttered.

A gentle chime echoed overhead, followed by a voice that sounded suspiciously like Benedict Cumberbatch whispering into a teacup.

"Welcome to your Companion Compatibility Audit. Please assume a position of spiritual openness."

Grace raised an eyebrow. "What does that mean?"

Leo immediately flopped belly-up on a meditation mat.

Grace sat cross-legged like a stressed-out schoolchild and tried not to panic.

* * *

A Bureau facilitator glided in — and yes, he really **glided**, as if wearing bureaucratically blessed socks — holding a clipboard that floated like it was judging her spine posture.

"Hello, I'm Gavin. I'll be overseeing your Empathic Bond Review today."

Gavin looked like a human IKEA candle: vaguely Scandinavian, smell-neutral, and too smooth to trust.

"We'll start with the Mirror Exercise," he said, clapping once. "Please look directly into each other's eyes and say the first adjective that comes to mind."

Grace turned to Leo, who stared at her with the serenity of someone who'd never paid taxes.

"...Stubborn," she said.

Leo tilted his head. "Frazzled."

Grace squinted. "Smug."

Leo purred. "Deflective."

Gavin beamed. "Wonderful! I sense a firm emotional dynamic. Now, please stand in the Circle of Truth."

* * *

The circle glowed as they stepped in.

A holographic voice echoed through the air.

"INITIATING BOND VULNERABILITY PROTOCOL. PLEASE STATE ONE FEAR."

"I'm afraid of being responsible for things I don't understand," Grace blurted.

Leo blinked.

"I'm afraid of being abandoned mid-mission because I'm inconvenient," he said after a pause.

The light flickered purple. Gavin's clipboard shivered approvingly.

"BONUS ROUND: PLEASE STATE ONE AFFECTIONATE MEMORY."

Grace was suddenly fourteen again, sitting with her childhood cat Luna under a blanket fort made of encyclopedias and teenage regret.

"...He reminds me of someone I lost," she said quietly.

Leo looked stunned.

"...She rubs my ears exactly the right way," he said.

The light went pink.

* * *

Then, without warning, a glowing ethereal screen appeared showing a scene from two days ago: Grace asleep on the sofa, mouth slightly open, one sock halfway off. Leo sat beside her, not touching her — just watching. For hours.

Grace went bright red.

Leo cleared his throat.

"Delete," he said.

"Nope," said Gavin. "That's gold. Now, for your final task — the Labyrinth of Mutual Compromise."

"What—"

But the floor dropped out before she could finish.

***

Inside the Labyrinth

Grace landed with an undignified *oof* on a glowing tile that pulsed like a passive-aggressive LED coaster. Leo landed on all fours like a smug ninja and immediately sat down to clean himself.

A sign floated into view:

"To Exit the Labyrinth, You Must Compromise."

The first hallway split in two:

- Left path: "Let Your Companion Make the Next Three Decisions."
- Right path: "Carry Your Companion for 200 Metres."

Grace glanced at Leo.

"I'm not carrying you."

"I'm not making three decisions."

They stared at each other.

Ten minutes later, Grace was piggybacking an eleven-kilogram tabby through a glittering fog of bureaucratic nonsense while muttering every complaint she'd ever had about government forms.

Leo offered no sympathy. But he did narrate.

"And so the human carried her emotional baggage in the shape of a moderately heavy sentient feline, wondering where her dignity had gone..."

Grace bumped him into a wall.

* * *

At the next checkpoint, a floating riddle blocked the exit.

"ONE OF YOU IS LYING. ONE OF YOU IS RIGHT. WHICH ONE TRUSTS THE OTHER MORE?"

Leo answered immediately. "She trusts me more."

Grace hesitated. "...Yeah. Probably."

The wall dissolved.

Behind it, a large golden orb hovered and announced:

"COMPATIBILITY SCORE: 84%. ROOM FOR GROWTH. LICENSING PERMITTED UNDER CLAUSE 6-WE-MIGHT-AS-WELL."

Gavin reappeared, sipping something fizzy and unlabelled.

"Congratulations," he said. "You've passed. Emotionally co-dependent, but stable enough for registration."

Leo looked smug. "Told you."

Grace muttered, "I still want a refund."

***

Interlude: The Orange Cat's Journal (Entry #05)

Emotional Audit Results:
- Not terrible
- Trust test survived
- Piggyback unpleasant but tolerable

Human vulnerability detected
- Past loss memory: registered
- Recurring guilt: unspoken
- Snack preference: banana bread (good taste)

Conclusion:
- I may, possibly, like this one
- She did not drop me in the labyrinth
- That means something

Next step:
- Submit results
- Pick up temporary license
- Convince her to buy more tuna

* * *

Part 3

The Gala of Initial Licensing

(also known — unofficially — as The Fancy But Deeply Confusing Ceremony)

Grace thought she was done once she passed the Compatibility Audit. But of course, that had only been the bureaucratic foreplay.

Now came the actual *event*.

"Why do I need to attend a ceremony for your paperwork?" she hissed at Leo as they stepped into what looked like a magical opera house crossed with a cat café and a mildly cursed museum.

Leo, now wearing a cravat ("It's enchanted silk. Don't wrinkle it."), looked around with barely concealed glee.

"Because," he said, "this is where we get **seen**. And once we're seen, the other departments can't easily delete us."

"That's comforting."

"Oh it's not," Leo said. "But it's strategy."

***

The room was packed.

Every row was filled with creatures and their humans — from sharp-eyed familiars perched on velvet cushions, to elegant foxes in waistcoats, to one very confused goose in a monocle.

A magical banner floated above the stage:

"Welcome, Provisional Companions! Please don't cast anything until called."

Grace sat beside Leo in the "Unbonded But Compliant" section.

On her other side sat a nervous-looking man with a glowing possum curled around his neck like an anxious scarf.

"I'm Geoff," he whispered. "This is Beatrice. She's technically extradimensional but only during full moons."

Grace nodded as though that made sense.

Leo rolled his eyes. "First-timers."

* * *

A hush fell.

The stage lights dimmed.

And from the swirling shadows emerged...

...a peacock.

A peacock in bifocals, with a badge that read **Senior Bureau Speaker** and a voice like a posh audiobook.

"Esteemed humans, familiars, and alternative sentients," he boomed. "Welcome to the Quarterly Companion Licensure Gala, Class 8-H."

Someone two rows up fainted. Possibly from the drama.

"We gather today not only to honour new provisional bonds, but to remind you all that **registration is a privilege, not a portal pass**. Bureau recognition may be temporary, but your obligations are eternal. Unless you shed your host body, in which case, please file Form 11-B."

Grace blinked. "What?!"

Leo whispered, "Ignore that. Bureau humour."

Grace wasn't sure what part of that was supposed to be funny.

***

Then the roll-call began.

Names were announced. Creatures stepped forward. There was clapping. There were glowing certificates. One chinchilla exploded into glitter and had to be reassembled by emergency sorcery.

Finally:

"Leo of the Unsorted Realms, Companion-Class (Pending), Anchor: Grace Harper."

Leo nudged her. "That's us."

They ascended the stairs, passing two arguing gargoyles and what looked like a levitating insurance agent.

The peacock bowed dramatically.

"Congratulations," he said. "You've survived the audit. You now face your final challenge."

Grace froze. "Excuse me, **what challenge**?"

Leo frowned. "That wasn't in the paperwork."

"Nothing ever is," the peacock replied. "This is a **real-time attunement test**. The Bureau wants to see if your bond holds under pressure."

"Define pressure."

The stage floor vanished.

* * *

They landed in... a fake living room?

It had floral wallpaper, tea stains on the carpet, and a mysteriously leaking ceiling.

A magical voice announced:

"SCENARIO: You have just found out your companion used your ID to order 43 cans of expensive interplanar tuna on your tab. What do you do?"

Grace turned to Leo.

He immediately said, "I regret nothing."

Grace folded her arms. "You have two seconds to convince me not to report you for fraud."

"I was hungry, and your budget lacks vision."

"Forty-three cans?!"

"They were on sale!"

***

Then the wall burst open.

A wave of flying bureaucratic forms flooded the room, swirling like angry origami.

"DEFEND YOUR BOND!" shouted the voice.

Leo hissed. "Get the scrolls!"

Grace dove into a pile of tax-like documentation, shielding Leo with her file folder. "I swear to every celestial department, if I get papercuts from a loyalty test—!"

A gust of magical wind knocked them off balance.

Leo leapt onto her shoulder. "Activate mutual trust!"

"How?!"

"Just say it!"

"I TRUST YOU NOT TO SPEND MY RENT MONEY ON FISH!"

The room glowed.

The storm paused.

The papers folded into a bouquet of apology flowers.

* * *

Back on stage, the crowd erupted into applause.

The peacock clucked. "Very touching. Mildly reckless. 8 out of 10. We'll file it under 'chaotic neutral with potential.'"

Grace was handed a scroll — warm to the touch and lightly purring.

Leo held it like a medal. "You're now officially part of the system."

Grace sighed. "I don't know whether to frame this or burn it."

Leo winked. "Do both. That's the bureaucratic spirit."

* * *

Interlude: The Orange Cat's Journal (Entry #06)

Ceremony Outcome:
- Survived theatrical registration ritual
- Got her to yell "I trust you" in front of 60 witnesses
- No visible mental breakdown (improvement)

Notes on Bureau:
- Peacock still has it
- Scenario engine malfunctioned (again)
- Chinchilla reassembled wrong (tail now speaks French)

Human Growth Index:
- Now understands magic events are 80% theatre
- Protective instincts activated
- Anger level = productive

Next Steps:
- Begin community integration
- Avoid Trevor for at least 48 hours
- Sleep in the clean laundry while pretending I don't care

* * *

Part 4

Welcome to the Neighbourhood, Again

Back in her flat, Grace opened the door, stepped inside, and dropped her Bureau-issued scroll directly onto a pile of unopened post.

Leo leapt onto the windowsill with practiced flair, tail flicking smugly.

"Officially licensed," he declared. "We should celebrate."

"You already celebrated. You ate an entire tin of commemorative trout pâté."

"I was being patriotic."

"You also made me yell 'I trust you' in front of an interdimensional audience."

Leo purred. "And you didn't burst into flames. Personal growth."

* * *

Grace slumped into her armchair, staring at the Bureau certificate that now hung crookedly on her wall.

It shimmered faintly, occasionally blinking like it might be alive.

She wasn't sure if that was normal or if she'd hung it too close to the microwave.

Her phone buzzed.

A message from the local community group chat lit up the screen:

Neighbourhood Watch: Magic Division
"New Companion Alert: Grace H. has completed licensing!
Welcome event in the courtyard tomorrow at 2pm. Attendance is mandatory unless you are temporarily incorporeal."

Grace groaned. "There's a party?"

Leo hopped down. "Oh yes. It's a rite of passage. Like a magical baby shower, but with more snacks and political subtext."

***

The Courtyard Carnival

The next day, the building courtyard looked like a magical village fête had collided with a Dungeons & Dragons fan convention.

Bunting spelled out *"WELCOME, GRADE-Q LIAISON HARPER & FELIFORM LEO"* in glowing, slightly passive-aggressive letters.

There was:

- A potion booth run by someone named "Margot, Level 2 Herbalist / Divorcee"
- A snack table guarded by what appeared to be an enchanted corgi
- And a "friendly duel zone" where a middle-aged man was challenging a sentient rabbit to a round of wandless insult combat.

Mrs. Netherby was already handing out lemon scones and whispering gossip at weaponised volume.

"She's the one with the talking cat, you know. The *orange one.*"

Trevor had set up a booth labelled:

"Leo Fan Club Applications: Now Accepting Gold, Art, or Praise"

Grace tried to disappear into a hedge.

Leo posed for three selfies and was offered a velvet cushion by a small hedgehog named Cyril.

***

Then a hush fell across the crowd.

Someone new had arrived.

A woman in a long grey coat stood by the gate, holding an umbrella despite clear skies. At her feet was a silver tabby with emerald eyes.

The cat froze when it saw Leo.

Leo froze back.

"Problem?" Grace asked, noting how still he'd gone.

Leo didn't answer. His ears twitched, tail low.

The silver tabby stepped forward. "You."

Leo exhaled. "Hello, *Vivienne*."

Grace blinked. "You... know each other?"

Vivienne sat elegantly. "Leo and I trained together. Before he vanished."

Leo glanced away. "Before I *escaped*, you mean."

* * *

Tension hummed like static.

Vivienne looked at Grace, eyes sharp. "He never told you what he was, did he?"

Grace folded her arms. "He said he was annoying and expensive."

Vivienne ignored that. "He used to be an **Archivist**."

Murmurs rippled through the crowd.

Cyril the Hedgehog fainted.

Leo muttered, "This is not the place."

Vivienne flicked her tail. "It never is. That's your excuse every time."

Trevor whispered to no one in particular, "I KNEW he had Archivist energy."

Grace stepped in. "Okay. What the hell is an Archivist?"

Vivienne's eyes narrowed. "Ask your cat. If he still remembers how to tell the truth."

* * *

Vivienne and her human vanished as suddenly as they'd come, leaving behind the scent of lavender and unresolved tension.

Leo sat down heavily on the pavement, staring into the middle distance.

Grace crouched beside him. "So. Archivist?"

He licked his paw without answering.

Grace nudged him. "Leo."

"I was part of the Bureau's Memory Division," he said eventually. "I archived magical trauma, companion separations, lost bonds. I recorded things that shouldn't be forgotten."

He looked at her, eyes less smug now.

"And then they tried to erase *me*."

* * *

The party awkwardly resumed.

Someone brought out cupcakes.

Trevor declared that "Leo's past lives only make him more qualified for leadership," and tried to start a parade.

Mrs. Netherby handed Grace a third scone and whispered, "Never trust a tabby with secrets."

Grace stood beside Leo, still processing.

"Why didn't you tell me?" she asked.

Leo glanced up at her. "Because the last person I told turned me in."

"Do you think I would?"

"I didn't know," he said. "Until today."

Grace sighed. "Well. Now we both have public shame trauma. Welcome to the neighbourhood."

Leo managed a soft purr. "We're bonding."

"Don't push it."

* * *

Interlude: The Orange Cat's Journal (Entry #07)

Public Event Outcome:
- Formal welcome = moderately humiliating
- Snacks = acceptable
- Emotional exposure = catastrophic

Vivienne Variable:
- Threat level: Emotional / Historical
- Possesses Bureau memory
- Likely watching from shadows

Anchor Reaction:
- Mild betrayal
- No immediate threats
- May still offer snacks

Next Steps:
- Disclose partial truth
- Avoid full explanation (for now)
- Sleep near front door, just in case

* * *

Part 5

Missing Cat, Missing Truth

That night, Grace woke up to find the window open and the cat gone.

Which was odd, considering she'd triple-locked it, charmed it shut with a Bureau-issued "Stay Inside" sigil, and pushed a bookshelf in front of it for good measure.

The only clue was a paw-drawn note scrawled on the back of her electricity bill:

"Gone for a walk. Don't panic. Or do. Whatever."

She stared at the paper.

Then she panicked.

* * *

After a brisk hunt through the neighbourhood (featuring one false alarm involving a sentient traffic cone and a very territorial raccoon), Grace turned to the only place Leo might go when emotionally compromised:

The **Neighbourhood Arcane Archive**, a semi-sentient library that only opened at night, only to registered familiars or deeply confused people with emotional baggage.

Grace qualified on both counts.

The door opened with a polite *creak* and a faint sigh.

Inside, it smelled of dust, forgotten emotions, and suspicious tea.

* * *

A floating index card greeted her:

"Welcome, Grace Harper.
Emotionally dishevelled, mildly qualified, potentially snoopy.
Please proceed to Room 7: Repressed Memory Annex."

She walked past shelves of glowing scrolls, a corridor labelled *"Unresolved Issues (Vol. II)"*, and what she was fairly sure was a whispering fern.

At the end of a flickering hallway, she found Leo.

Sitting under a floating orb, staring at a screen made of light, memory, and regret.

He didn't turn around.

"They tried to wipe me," he said.

Grace stepped closer. "Who?"

"The Bureau. The Archivist Division. I knew too much. I remembered things they wanted lost."

The orb flickered and replayed a scene:

A younger Leo — slightly smaller, less orange — comforting a child weeping beside a glowing cat carrier.

Another scene:

Leo recording a dying phoenix's final thoughts in a crystalline journal.

Another:

Leo arguing with a tabby in a grey coat.

Vivienne.

***

"I refused an order," he said. "They wanted me to erase the bond record of a Companion who'd defected. I said no. So they made me disappear."

He looked at her now.

"I don't remember her name. They took it. But the rest? They couldn't reach."

Grace sat down beside him.

"I believe you."

Leo blinked. "You do?"

"You eat flowers, you sass strangers, you nap in my clean laundry. But you don't lie. Not about this."

He swallowed. "You're the first to say that."

A soft chime rang.

"Emotional resonance confirmed," the library whispered.
"New shelf unlocked: Shared Record (Anchor Class)."

* * *

A door appeared in the wall.

Grace and Leo entered together.

Inside was a single book, hovering midair.

It was blank.

Then words appeared, one by one:

"Harper & Leo: Companion Record. Status — Developing. Primary Bond Emotion: Reluctant Loyalty, Emerging Trust."

Leo tilted his head. "We're... official again."

Grace reached out. "We never weren't."

The book purred.

* * *

They walked home in silence, Leo curled around her shoulders like a ginger scarf of unresolved trauma.

At her door, he paused.

"Would you be angry if I said this is bigger than either of us?"

"I'd be angrier if you said it wasn't."

He nodded.

Then added: "Also, the raccoon down the street has a crush on your bike."

Grace sighed. "Of course she does."

* * *

Interlude: The Orange Cat's Journal (Entry #08)

Status:
- Memory retrieval: partial
- Truth shared: selective
- Anchor response: unexpectedly supportive

Library outcome:
- New bond shelf created
- Emotionally messy, archivally sound

Risks:
- Vivienne may report
- Bureau eyes may return

Recommendations:
- Stay close
- Stay sarcastic
- Stay ready

* * *

Part 6

The Bureau Wants a Word (and Possibly a Blood Sample)

On Monday, Grace received another scroll — this one delivered by a flaming squirrel with an ID badge.

She barely blinked anymore.

The scroll read:

MANDATORY DEBRIEFING NOTICE
Your companion has been flagged for archival irregularities.
Please attend a Discreet Reintegration Dialogue (DRD) at Bureau Substation 9½.
Time: Now.
Dress code: Yes.

Leo read it over her shoulder. "Oh good. They're using euphemisms again."

" 'Discreet Reintegration Dialogue' sounds like a cult-themed escape room."

"Just say no to blood-letting," Leo offered helpfully.

Substation 9½: A Place That Definitely Smelled Like Guilt

Grace arrived wearing her best "I'm just a civilian with too many questions" expression and a blouse that hadn't been ironed since 2020.

Leo was in her tote bag, loudly pretending to be a very fancy loaf of bread.

The receptionist looked bored until Grace said the word "archival."

Then she was escorted immediately to a room with soundproof walls, three magical lie-detection sigils, and a chair that adjusted itself to be slightly less comfortable the longer she sat in it.

Across the table sat **Agent Ferrow**, a man who looked like someone had tried to sculpt "stern" out of chalk.

※ ※ ※

"Ms. Harper," he said. "Do you know the full nature of your companion?"

Grace tilted her head. "I'm pretty sure he's 80% fur, 10% ego, and 10% expired sardine pâté."

Ferrow didn't smile.

"You're aware he was once classified as an Archivist-Level Three?"

"I am now."

"Are you aware of the rules around memory tampering?"

"I've had to fill out five forms just to remember what day it is. So yes."

Ferrow leaned forward. "He should not exist."

Grace blinked. "Well, tough. He does. And he snores."

"He carries knowledge sealed after the Claremont Split."

That gave her pause.

Leo, still loafed in her tote, muttered, "Of course they'd bring that up."

Grace asked slowly, "What is the Claremont Split?"

Ferrow glanced at the sigils on the wall.

"Redacted," he said. "But you don't want to be involved. Return the cat."

* * *

Grace crossed her arms.

"No."

"You'll be monitored."

"Join the queue."

"He may put your reality at risk."

"Then I'll wear goggles."

Ferrow exhaled hard enough to disturb the air enchantment.

"I'm putting you under Tier-Three Scrutiny."

"Will there be a badge?"

Ferrow blinked. "What?"

"Because I'd like a badge."

Even Leo snorted.

* * *

Outside, Grace didn't speak until they reached a crosswalk that blinked purple and said "It's Emotionally Safe to Proceed."

Then she looked down at Leo.

"Claremont?"

He stared straight ahead. "An event. A fracture. A seal."

"You were there."

"I might've been part of it."

"Why didn't you tell me?"

Leo's voice dropped. "Because if you know too much... they might try to erase *you* too."

Grace swallowed.

Then knelt beside him.

"You're not alone in this."

Leo met her gaze.

"You really want to know the truth?"

"I've already attended a memory-based obstacle course and yelled 'I trust you' in public. I'm pot-committed."

Leo sighed.

"Then we'll start tonight."

***

Interlude: The Orange Cat's Journal (Entry #09)

Bureau Status:
- Flagged
- Interrogated
- Threatened (mildly)

Anchor Behaviour:
- Defensive
- Snarky
- Loyal

Next Actions:
- Reveal partial Claremont history
- Avoid Agent Ferrow
- Eat emotional support fish treats

***

Part 7

Fragments and Fish Biscuits

That night, Leo didn't nap.

Which, for him, was a major red flag. Nap avoidance was equivalent to a full mental breakdown in cat language.

Instead, he sat on the kitchen counter, staring at the dimly glowing kettle as if it might answer for his past sins.

Grace, for once, didn't push.

She placed a tin of anchovy biscuits on the table and waited.

Leo jumped down, sniffed the tin, ignored it, then sighed.

"Claremont," he began, "wasn't supposed to happen. It was a dimensional convergence event. Accidental. Mostly."

Grace leaned forward.

"There was... an experiment. Trying to stabilise fractured realities. We Archivists were meant to document the risk, not intervene."

His tail twitched.

"But I did."

* * *

The orb from the library flickered back into view, summoned by unspoken memory.

It projected a new scene.

Leo, younger, arguing with a trio of robed figures. One wore an emblem: the **Eye of the Outer Index**.

"She wasn't supposed to go!" Leo shouted in the vision. "She was my anchor—she *trusted* us!"

"They all trust," said one figure. "That's what makes them usable."

Grace clenched her fists. "They sacrificed someone."

Leo nodded. "And when I refused to archive her erasure, they tried to erase me."

Another memory fragment: Leo, in the archives, pulling runes from a wall and running through a collapsing portal.

The image faded.

* * *

"You still don't remember her name?" Grace asked softly.

"I remember her laugh," he said. "And that she made terrible mushroom soup."

He looked at her. "That's why I don't trust the Bureau."

Grace looked at the glowing scroll on her wall — now noticeably dimmer.

"They're watching us."

Leo nodded. "But they can't control us if we bond fully."

Grace frowned. "Like... magic marriage?"

"More like magical co-signing a mortgage of cosmic responsibility."

"Oh great," she muttered. "Cat bureaucracy plus commitment."

Leo paused.

"I can undo it later," he offered. "But if we do it now — they'll have to register us as a **Tier-One Companion Pair**. No more interference."

Grace stood up.

"Let's do it."

***

The Bonding

They stood in the centre of the living room.

Leo placed a paw on her shoe.

"Repeat after me," he said solemnly.

"I, Grace Harper—"

"I, Grace Harper—"

"Do solemnly promise not to sell my Companion's secrets to the tabloids."

Grace blinked.

Leo smirked. "Just checking. Here's the real one."

They both recited the vow:

"By thread of trust and shared chaos,
I bind this bond in mutual nonsense and necessary loyalty.
May paperwork favour us,
and cosmic stupidity ignore us."

A soft golden light enveloped them.

For a moment, Grace felt her heartbeat slow, then match the calm pulse of Leo's. Not intrusive. Just... steady.

Shared.

* * *

A chime rang.

Then silence.

On the wall, the Bureau certificate reshaped itself.

New text appeared in bold script:

Harper & Leo
Tier-One Companion Pair (Unorthodox Subcategory)
Approved under Clause 13-C (Low Risk of Interdimensional Collapse)

Leo collapsed onto the carpet.

Grace sat beside him.

"You okay?" she asked.

Leo yawned. "That was emotionally exhausting. Also, I'm hungry."

Grace opened the biscuit tin.

He immediately pretended he hadn't been emotionally available five minutes ago.

*　*　*

Outside, a figure watched from a nearby rooftop.

Vivienne.

She tapped a crystal communicator.

"Confirmation," she said. "The bond is sealed."

A pause.

Then: "Yes. He's remembering.
No. I didn't interfere.
Yes... for now."

She faded into the fog like all dramatically inclined cats tend to do.

* * *

Interlude: The Orange Cat's Journal (Entry #10)

Bond Status:
- Tier One
- Mutual
- Possibly emotional

Grace Notes:
- Said the vow
- Didn't run
- May make decent soup

Complication Risk:
- Vivienne tracking
- Bureau divided
- Claremont resonance: increasing

Conclusion:
- She's not her
- But she might be enough

Immediate Priority:
- Sleep
- Snacks

- Pretend this isn't the beginning of something enormous

Chapter Three: Three Letters and a Formal Affair

* * *

An Officially Ridiculous Requirement

The next morning, Grace opened her letterbox and found a bureaucratic pigeon staring at her.

It cooed in tones that implied it had a clipboard somewhere.

Attached to its leg was a scroll tied in gold twine and passive-aggressive bureaucracy.

"To: Grace Harper & Companion Leo
From: Bureau of Companion Continuity and Feline Affairs
Subject: Permanent Integration Application (Form 17-C: Long-Term Companion Licensing)

NOTICE: In accordance with Bureau Clause 27-R (Civic Social Verification), you are required to obtain THREE recommendation letters from registered catfolk or citizens:

1. One unmarried
2. One married
3. One divorced

Letters must be emotionally sincere and notarised by someone vaguely magical.

Deadline: Next Tuesday.

Failure to comply will result in reclassification under "Feral Entanglement.""

Grace looked up.

The pigeon saluted and vanished in a puff of lavender-scented logic.

Leo appeared behind her, stretching.

"Oh good," he said. "We're back to hoops."

* * *

The Hunt Begins

Grace groaned. "Why do we need letters from people based on *marital status?*"

Leo hopped onto the kitchen counter. "Because the Bureau believes cats are best judged by the company they keep, and the chaos they survive."

"So we need someone single, someone legally entangled, and someone traumatised."

"Exactly. And they must all like me enough to write something flowery."

"You are *barely* likable."

He purred. "Which makes this more fun."

* * *

Grace opened her Community Magic Directory — an enchanted pamphlet bound by spell glue and mild passive aggression.

She flipped to the section labelled:

"Neighbourhood Cats (Sentient / Occasionally Romantic)"

Names shimmered across the page:

- Trevor, unmarried, socially problematic
- Romina & Baxter (married, mildly cursed)
- Miss Elsie (divorced, twice, possibly homicidal)

Leo licked his paw. "I say we start with the easy one."

Grace blinked. "Which is that?"

He grinned. "The divorced cat lady."

* * *

Part 1

The Divorced Letter – Tea with Miss Elsie

Miss Elsie lived in Flat 5B, a two-bedroom fortress guarded by seventeen porcelain owls, a cactus that occasionally screamed, and the smell of unresolved bitterness.

She answered the door in a lavender dressing gown and eyeliner sharp enough to puncture ego.

"Harper," she said, "and the orange disappointment."

"Good afternoon," Grace said politely.

Elsie squinted. "What do you want? If it's about the garden gnome incident, I have legal immunity."

Grace held up the scroll.

"We need a letter."

Elsie scanned it.

"Divorced category. Of course." She turned to Leo. "Still smuggling fish guts into my hydrangeas?"

"I've matured," Leo lied.

She huffed. "Fine. But I want something in return."

Grace blinked. "Like what?"

"I need you," Elsie said, "to pretend to be my legal witness tomorrow."

"...To what?"

"My ex is renewing his vows with his new wife. And I intend to attend."

Leo grinned. "You're a villain. I respect it."

* * *

The next day was a melodrama with canapés.

Miss Elsie, dressed like a widow who'd outlived spite itself, arrived late, loud, and heavily perfumed.

She took Grace's arm and whispered, "Say nothing. Just look like you disapprove of everything."

Grace nailed it.

Leo, who'd snuck in inside a handbag, meowed once during the vows.

Miss Elsie clapped politely.

Then left a signed scroll on the cake table.

"To whom it may concern:
The cat Leo is a chaotic force of nature. Anyone who can survive him deserves Bureau protection and probably a medal.

(P.S. He still owes me a lawn ornament.)
— Miss Elsie, twice divorced, once dramatic."

* * *

Back at home, Grace pinned the first letter to the fridge.

"Next?"

Leo yawned. "The married couple. But we may need to break into their attic first."

Grace froze. "Why?"

He looked innocently smug. "Because I may have accidentally redirected a minor scam spell into their chimney."

Grace facepalmed. "Of course you did."

* * *

Part 2

The Married Letter — Domestic Magic Is a Trap

Romina and Baxter lived in the flat directly above Grace — a fact she was reminded of every Sunday when they practiced something called "passive-aggressive flamenco" at 8 a.m.

They were, by all outward appearances, blissfully married: matching bathrobes, matching teacups, and a talking toaster that addressed them both as "my darlings."

Leo had described them as "surprisingly stable for people who once hexed a council planner."

Grace stood at their door now, clutching a tub of lemon tarts and trying to look apologetic.

Romina opened it. Her eyebrows immediately lifted.

"Leo," she said. "Here to confess something?"

Leo tried a sheepish smile. "Maybe."

Baxter joined her, holding a hammer that glowed faintly.

"Oh dear," Grace said. "That's never a good sign."

* * *

Romina led them inside.

The living room was neat, cheerful, and very slightly humming — as though the walls were trying to hold in a secret.

"So," Baxter said, setting down the hammer, "let's talk about the scam."

Grace blinked. "Wait. There was an actual scam?"

Romina nodded. "Someone enchanted our smart doorbell. Every time we opened the front door, we were agreeing to a new magical subscription."

Leo winced.

"Right," he said. "That may have been my fault."

"You redirected the protection rune into our perimeter," Romina said. "Which is clever, if deeply unethical."

"It was Tuesday," Leo said. "I was improvising."

Baxter sighed. "Well, now our flat is spiritually signed up to: three energy crystals, one mentorship retreat in a dream dimension, and a sentient bread subscription."

Grace raised a hand. "I don't mean to interrupt the incredibly surreal argument, but—how can we help?"

Romina pointed upwards.

"The attic is now sealed with a binding contract. We can't go in, because we're legally listed as 'romantically compromised parties' in the subscription agreement."

Leo whistled. "Damn. That's binding."

* * *

The Attic of Interpersonal Doom

The attic hatch glowed purple. A sign read:

"ATTIC ACCESS DENIED:
EMOTIONAL ENTANGLEMENT LEVEL: 87%
CONFLICT: WHO LEFT THE LAUNDRY IN THE DRYER
SUGGESTED ACTION: Mediate or separate."

"Wow," Grace muttered. "Magic *really* wants you to go to couple's therapy."

Romina handed her a wand-like object. "This is the Remote Unentanglement Key. You'll have to go in and deactivate the enchantment. Try not to look at the memories. They get nosy."

Leo hopped on her shoulder. "I'll guide."

"Do you know the layout?" Grace asked.

"I lived up here for three weeks," Leo said. "I was hiding from a disillusioned chinchilla sorcerer. Don't ask."

* * *

Inside, the attic felt like an emotional pressure cooker.

Every object buzzed with suppressed arguments and passive-aggressive energy.

On a dusty dresser, a mug read:

"I'M NOT MAD, I'M JUST ENCHANTED THAT WAY."

Grace tiptoed past a glowing yoga mat, a self-writing grocery list (currently stuck on *"more boundaries"*), and a sentient tax return that hissed, "Leave while you still can."

At the centre sat a crystal box. Inside: a contract scroll glowing bright red.

Leo peered at it. "Yup. That's the Subscription Core. Touch it wrong and it'll replay every romantic disappointment you've ever witnessed."

"Excellent," Grace muttered. "I've seen my parents try to buy IKEA furniture together. I'm immune."

She tapped the scroll with the wand.

A gentle *ding* echoed. The room calmed.

* * *

Back downstairs, Romina and Baxter looked visibly lighter.

"We can go near the fridge without arguing now," Baxter said.

"We feel spiritually re-synced," Romina added.

Leo made a gagging sound.

Grace cleared her throat. "So... about that letter?"

Romina handed her a gold-inked scroll.

"To Whom It May Concern:
We, Romina and Baxter of Flat 6A, hereby affirm that the feline Leo is a manipulative, self-interested creature who nevertheless managed to help us resolve magical subscription entanglement.

His companion, Grace Harper, is either incredibly brave or permanently exhausted. Either way, we support their union.

Signed with emotional clarity and matching handwriting."

Grace took it with relief.

Two down. One to go.

She turned to Leo.

"Now for the unmarried witness. You thinking who I'm thinking?"

Leo grimaced. "God help us, it's Trevor time."

* * *

Interlude: The Orange Cat's Journal (Entry #11)

Letter Status:

✓ Divorced — Obtained via emotional sabotage

✓ Married — Obtained via magical attic purge

-- Unmarried — Pending (Trevor-shaped disaster)

Human Notes:
– Crawled through attic of marital horror without screaming
– Resisted urge to edit the grocery list
– Still giving me the side-eye about everything

Next Step:
– Bribe, distract, or survive Trevor
– Possibly all three

* * *

Part 3

The Unmarried Letter — Trevor's Cat-tastrophe

Trevor lived in Flat 3C and self-identified as a "Feline Visionary, Social Disruptor, and Emotional Influencer."

He also wore bow ties that changed colour based on his mood. Currently: salmon pink — dangerously optimistic.

Grace knocked. The door flew open as if it had been waiting to be dramatic.

"Grace!" Trevor beamed. "I sensed you were coming. The wind told me."

Leo sighed. "That was me sneezing outside your air vent."

"No difference," Trevor said grandly, stepping aside. "Please, enter the Temple of Solitude and Mild Desperation."

The flat smelled like citrus, incense, and existential thirst.

Every visible surface featured a framed inspirational quote. One read:

"You are not single. You are in a relationship with infinite possibility."

Another said:

"Just because they have fur doesn't mean they can't hurt you."

* * *

Trevor gestured to a velvet couch shaped like a question mark.

"So! What brings you here? Advice? Auras? Emotional clarity?"

Grace cleared her throat. "We need a letter. Unmarried category. For the Bureau."

Trevor gasped. "Oh my goodness, it's happening. You want *my* validation?!"

Leo muttered, "Technically, we want your handwriting."

Trevor flopped dramatically onto the couch. "Fine. But I don't give away bureaucratic credibility for free. There must be... an exchange."

Grace braced herself. "What kind of exchange?"

Trevor sat up, eyes gleaming.

"You help me run my First Annual Magical Singles Mingle."

Leo nearly fell off the windowsill. "That's a real thing?!"

"Oh yes," Trevor whispered. "And it's tonight."

* * *

The Singles Mingle (AKA Magical Speed Dating with Snacks)

The venue: a repurposed potion workshop.
The vibe: chaotic optimism and too many string lights.

There were stations for "Shared Potion Mixing," "Charm Compatibility Games," and a mystical compatibility wheel that kept bursting into flames.

Grace was handed a clipboard, a whistle, and a sash that read:

"MINGLE FACILITATOR: ASK ME ABOUT EMOTIONAL RISK"

Leo wore a bowtie that changed colour every 90 seconds to "enhance emotional perception."

"This is a circus," Grace muttered.

"This is a *vibe*," Trevor corrected, bustling past with a tray of aphrodisiac macarons.

* * *

First pair of daters:

- A one-eyed tabby with commitment issues.
- A ghost ferret seeking spiritual closure.

They argued over rent.

Second pair:

- A telepathic crow.
- A marmalade cat who only spoke in Elizabethan English.

They hit it off alarmingly well.

Leo observed from a high perch, munching macaron crumbs.

"This is more emotionally honest than most Bureau interviews."

"True," Grace said. "But I'm still making everyone sign waivers."

* * *

Halfway through the night, Trevor rang a ceremonial bell.

"Time for the final group exercise: **Reveal Your Magical Wound!**"

Everyone groaned.

Grace marched up to him. "You said nothing about wounds."

Trevor smiled. "Everyone's broken, darling. Might as well network through it."

* * *

One brave soul stood up.

"I was once bonded to a familiar who turned out to be three raccoons in a trench coat."

Gasps.

Another whispered, "I still dream of the frog who left."

Leo leaned over to Grace. "You should share. It'll humanise you."

"I'm already drowning in weird."

He nuzzled her arm. "You're doing great."

She didn't say anything, but she didn't elbow him either.

Progress.

* * *

The Final Letter

At the end of the evening, as the last enchanted cupcake collapsed into glitter and someone slow-danced with a broom, Trevor approached with a scroll sealed in glitter wax.

"To the Esteemed Bureau:
Leo is emotionally unavailable but deeply effective.
His human, Grace, is proof that love can be built on chaos, consent, and shared snacks.

I, Trevor of 3C, unmarried by choice and sometimes delusion, support their registration with *flair*."

Grace took the scroll.

"Thank you," she said.

Trevor dabbed at his eyes. "I knew love could be administratively supported."

* * *

Interlude: The Orange Cat's Journal (Entry #12)

Letter Status:

√ Divorced – Secured through petty vengeance

√ Married – Secured through attic therapy

√ Unmarried – Secured through public matchmaking

Bond Status:
– Now verifiably endorsed
– Likely being watched
– Emotionally ridiculous

Anchor Note:
– Still here

– Still stubborn

– Might even like me (pending snacks)

**

Part 4

The Verification Ceremony (a.k.a. The Paperwork Lie Detector)

Three scrolls.

Each signed, sealed, and slightly crinkled from being kept in Grace's handbag between packets of gum and a slightly angry lemon.

She placed them reverently on the marble counter of the Bureau's Companion Verification Kiosk — a structure that looked like a church confessional had crashed into an office supplies store.

The Bureau clerk, a floating jellyfish in a bowler hat, jiggled approvingly.

"Excellent," it said in a calming, gurgling tone. "Now, we shall perform the **Sincerity Verification Ritual**."

Grace blinked. "Sorry, what now?"

The jellyfish extended a tentacle toward a glowing orb labeled:

SINCER-O-METER 3000™

Now with 15% more passive aggression!

* * *

Each letter was fed into the orb.

A beam of light scanned the page.

Then a robotic voice echoed from the orb:

"Processing Emotional Sincerity...

Letter One: Miss Elsie...

73% genuine. 12% petty. 15% theatrically vindictive.
Classification: ACCEPTED."

Leo snorted. "She'll love that breakdown."

"Letter Two: Romina & Baxter...

82% genuine. 10% sarcastic. 8% residual potion fumes.
Classification: ACCEPTED."

Grace exhaled.

"Letter Three: Trevor...

...calibrating... recalibrating...
Emotional sincerity: 51%. Glitter density: 440%.

Passive flirtation: HIGH.

Classification: **Pending Further Review**."

Grace groaned. "Of course."

* * *

The jellyfish floated slightly lower in an expression of bureaucratic concern.

"Regrettably," it said, "Letter Three requires manual validation."

"What does that even mean?" Grace asked.

"Your third recommender must attend a Bureau-sanctioned **Sincerity Summit**, where their emotional motivations will be judged by a panel of magical notaries, retired relationship counsellors, and one freelance poet."

Leo facepawed. "The Bureau is a theatre company disguised as a government."

Grace sighed. "And if Trevor refuses?"

The jellyfish jiggled. "You must provide a substitute unmarried recommender with higher sincerity metrics."

Leo leaned toward Grace. "We could ask the hedgehog."

Grace blinked. "Cyril?"

"He once gave me a daisy and told me I radiate complex energy. That's basically a marriage proposal in his culture."

* * *

Meanwhile: Vivienne Returns

Later that evening, Grace sat on her balcony, contemplating her life decisions, when Vivienne appeared like a regret in silk — poised, unreadable, and accompanied by a silver breeze.

"You're progressing," she said, as if complimenting a houseplant.

Leo appeared beside Grace, tail twitching. "Still lurking, I see."

Vivienne ignored him. "Has she seen the memories yet?"

Grace frowned. "I've seen fragments."

"Then you've only seen the shadows."

Leo narrowed his eyes. "This isn't your jurisdiction anymore."

Vivienne tilted her head. "Isn't it? You're still a loose thread, Leo. And loose threads attract unravelers."

Grace stood. "Enough riddles. What do you want?"

Vivienne's eyes gleamed.

"To help you survive what's coming."

***

Interlude: The Orange Cat's Journal (Entry #13)

Verification Status:

– Two letters: Approved

– Trevor's: Under Review (of course)

– Bureau Orb: Judgemental

Vivienne Status:

– Increasingly cryptic

– Possibly helpful

– Definitely annoying

Anchor Mood:

– Frustrated

– Sassy

– Determined

Next Actions:

– Choose: Cyril or Confront Trevor

– Consider showing Grace the full memory archive

– Steal fish

***

Part 5

Trevor's Trial of Truth (and Sparkles)

Two days later, Grace found herself seated inside the Bureau's *Sincerity Dome*, a transparent bubble suspended above a koi pond that whispered personal insecurities when you walked past it.

Trevor was seated across from her on a floating dais, surrounded by a trio of magical adjudicators.

They included:

- A retired enchantment lawyer named Glenda, who wore a judicial wig shaped like a beehive.
- A ghostly relationship therapist from 1823 named Dr. Winslow.
- And a freelance spoken-word poet named Mist ("Just Mist, no surname, please").

Leo, sitting beside Grace, whispered, "I give this circus a six out of ten already."

A bell rang.

Glenda called the room to order.

"Mr. Trevor of 3C, are you emotionally sincere in your recommendation of one Leo, feline, and Grace Harper, anchor class?"

Trevor rose, placed his paw dramatically over his heart, and said, "I speak only truths. And occasionally interpretive dance."

Mist clapped quietly.

* * *

A glowing orb floated down from the dome ceiling.

"This is the Veritasphere," Winslow intoned. "It will amplify your inner truth. If you lie, it will squeak."

Trevor cleared his throat.

"Leo is... orange."

The orb glowed a steady blue.

"Leo is also... emotionally complicated."

Still blue.

"Leo once ate half of my birthday cake and blamed the wind."

The orb pulsed purple.

Leo muttered, "It *was* windy."

Trevor inhaled.

"Grace Harper is loyal, resilient, and possibly half-wizard, I haven't ruled it out."

The orb turned pink and emitted a gentle *ding*.

Glenda scribbled something on a scroll.

Trevor finished: "Their bond is real. Messy, perhaps. Weird, absolutely. But real."

The orb played a soothing harp chord.

* * *

Mist stood, clearly moved.

"I feel seen," they whispered. "And also slightly hungry."

Winslow nodded. "I declare this testimony... sufficiently earnest."

Glenda stamped the scroll.

"Letter Three: APPROVED.
Status: Sincerity Level 86%.
Passive flirtation: High but legal."

Trevor bowed, nearly tripping over his own tail.

Grace exhaled. "Finally."

Leo purred. "One less hoop. And Trevor's ego survives intact."

* * *

Back at Home: Trouble Brews in Teacups

That evening, the scrolls glowed gently on Grace's kitchen table — all three, now Bureau-certified and laminated by what appeared to be magical humidity.

Leo lounged on the windowsill, chewing on a quill.

Grace leaned back in her chair, halfway through her second cinnamon tea of the evening.

"We did it," she said. "Three letters, ridiculous as they were."

Leo nodded. "So naturally, something awful will happen now."

She frowned. "Do you *have* to say that out loud?"

"Just getting ahead of the narrative arc."

At that exact moment, the lights flickered.

The kettle screamed.

And a mysterious envelope slipped under the door.

* * *

Grace picked it up cautiously.

It was sealed with a wax sigil she didn't recognise — a spiral within a spiral, surrounded by ink-black leaves.

Leo's eyes narrowed.

"That's not Bureau."

Grace opened it. The parchment inside read:

"To Grace Harper and Leo,

You've passed the test set by *them*.
Now let's see how you handle *us*.

— O."

Grace turned it over.

Nothing else.

Leo said nothing for a long while.

Then, quietly, "It's starting."

* * *

Interlude: The Orange Cat's Journal (Entry #14)

Letter Status:

✓ Approved

Bureau Status:
— Temporarily appeased
— Likely suspicious

Unknown Factor:
— The Letter from O
— Spiral sigil = ancient, pre-Bureau faction
— Possibly Observers… or worse

Grace Response:
— Calm
— Sharp
— Still drinking tea

Next Step:
— Prepare for the invitation
— Watch the shadows
— Sleep on her laptop

* * *

Part 6

The Letter from O (a.k.a. the Invitation That Shouldn't Exist)

The parchment burned itself precisely seven minutes after being opened — bursting into silent, odourless flame and vanishing without a trace, leaving behind only a faint smell of possibility.

Grace stared at the empty floor.

Leo said nothing.

Then, slowly: "We shouldn't answer it."

Grace raised an eyebrow. "That's cute. You think I'm going to *not* follow the mysterious flaming clue?"

He sighed. "Of course not. Curiosity is the human version of tail-chasing."

"Besides," she said, grabbing her jacket, "they already know where we live. Might as well RSVP with flair."

***

The letter hadn't said where to go.

But the back of Grace's hand now glowed faintly, like a magically indecisive tattoo.

It pulsed gently whenever she pointed it toward the Baker Street Underground station.

Leo clung to her shoulder like a ginger satellite dish, guiding her through increasingly improbable turns, side corridors, and at least one false wall hidden behind a decorative vending machine.

Eventually, they reached an abandoned lift shaft.

Above it, graffiti in ancient rune script read:

"Those who seek the unspoken must first descend below the conveniently ignored."

The lift creaked to life on its own.

Naturally.

* * *

The Club Below London

At the bottom was a door shaped like a sideways question mark.

Leo sniffed. "Illusion magic. And mahogany. Classy."

The door opened into a long hallway lit with glowing lanterns, each flickering to a rhythm only emotionally available people could probably hear.

At the end was a grand room that looked like a cross between a Victorian salon, a forgotten museum, and a cat café that took itself *way too seriously.*

A dozen figures looked up as Grace entered.

One wore a monocle on their ear.

Another sipped tea from a levitating cup that corrected grammar as you drank.

A third, the only one who smiled, stepped forward.

They were tall, androgynous, wearing a coat made of stitched-up maps.

"Welcome," they said. "You've passed the Bureau's test. But that was the easy part."

Grace crossed her arms. "And you are?"

"I am Oberon," they said, voice soft and dangerous. "One of the Watchers. The ones who see what the Bureau won't."

Leo hissed. "You're not supposed to be here."

Oberon tilted their head. "Neither are you. And yet…"

***

Unlicensed Truth

The Watchers called themselves **The Uncatalogued**.

They were former Bureau members, rogue archivists, memory specialists, and anomaly chasers — the ones who had refused to erase, redact, or forget.

They'd been exiled from the Bureau's records.

But not from reality.

Oberon led Grace and Leo to a table carved from petrified thought.

He laid down a scroll.

"Claremont was a containment," he said. "A spell to hold what should never have been touched. But it cracked. And someone — something — slipped through."

Grace felt a chill that had nothing to do with temperature.

Leo stared. "You think I brought it?"

"We think you bonded with it."

***

Oberon turned to Grace.

"You've seen fragments. But if we help you see the whole — if we unlock him — you might not come back the same."

Leo growled. "Don't push her."

Grace looked between them.

"If I *don't* look?"

"Then eventually, it will use you without asking."

That did it.

Grace nodded.

"Show me."

* * *

Oberon placed a ring of obsidian glass on the table. "Touch this. Think of Leo. And hold on."

Grace reached out.

The world went sideways.

* * *

Fragment: The Memory Vault

She stood in a memory not her own.

Leo — younger, sharper, wild — stood beside a girl. Her hair was like ash, her laugh full of fire.

Grace's heart skipped.

That was... not her.

The girl whispered: "They'll come for me."

Leo said: "Then we go first."

Another flash.

The girl collapsed. Leo screamed. Runes exploded.

A clawed shadow loomed.

Then—

The vision shattered.

* * *

Back in the room, Grace gasped.

Leo steadied her with a paw on her wrist.

"You saw her," he said.

She nodded. "She loved you."

He looked away. "She was my anchor."

Grace whispered, "And now?"

He looked back.

"You might be my second chance."

* * *

Interlude: The Orange Cat's Journal (Entry #15)

Letter Status:

✓ All done

Unknown Invitation:
– Accepted
– Regretted
– Understood

Anchor Reaction:
– Brave
– Not broken
– Still here

Self Status:
– Memory integration: unstable
– Emotional availability: fluctuating
– Danger level: rising

Conclusion:

– We're in it now

– I can't lose her

– Not again

* * *

Part 7

The Cat, the Code, and the Catastrophe That's Coming

The moment they stepped out of the Watchers' subterranean lair, Grace's phone — previously useless in magical zones — lit up with seventeen notifications from the Bureau.

She opened the first.

Bureau Alert: Companion Bond #1478
Anomaly detected. Magic saturation beyond acceptable thresholds.
Compliance request issued. Location pinged.
Agent dispatched.

You have been flagged for Proactive Review.

Leo read over her shoulder and hissed, "We're now officially in the pre-criminal category."

Grace kept scrolling.

Attached: One (1) Final Review Invitation
Location: Bureau Tier Clearance Hall
Time: Tomorrow, Noon
Required Attire: Emotionally Appropriate

She groaned. "What does that *even* mean?"

Leo deadpanned, "Wear something between 'funeral of a conscience' and 'surprise tax audit.'"

* * *

The Night Before the Review

Grace couldn't sleep.

Leo paced the windowsill like a feline thundercloud.

They both kept almost saying something.

Finally, Grace broke the silence.

"What if the Bureau decides to unpair us?"

Leo didn't look at her. "They can't. The bond is sealed."

"Bureau override clause?"

He sighed. "There's always a clause."

She sat up. "We have to be ready."

"For what?" Leo asked.

She looked out the window, into the kind of London night that felt two degrees off from reality.

"For everything."

* * *

Meanwhile, at Bureau HQ, a figure in white gloves closed a folder marked:

Case 1478: Leo & Anchor Harper

Recommended Outcome: Pending Claremont Protocol Review

"Bring in the anchor," the figure whispered.

"No more testing.
This time... we extract."

* * *

Interlude: The Orange Cat's Journal (Entry #16)

Status:
— Letters: Complete
— Bureau: Alarmed
— Watchers: Interfering

Anchor Mood:

– Not afraid

– Not naïve

– Dangerous, in the best way

Me:

– Memories unsealing

– Core resonance unstable

– Feeling things

Tomorrow's Plan:

– Walk in like we belong

– Smile like it's fine

– Bring snacks

* * *

Part 8

Final Review (Now With Extra Existential Peril)

Grace stood in the middle of the Bureau's Tier Clearance Hall, which felt less like a government office and more like the waiting room of an ancient, omniscient god who didn't believe in comfortable chairs.

Around her, the walls pulsed with spell-scripts and slow-moving bureaucratic thoughts like:

"Form 82b-A is emotionally incomplete."
"Your intentions will now be reviewed. Please remain delusionally calm."

Leo perched beside her, unusually quiet.

"Any last-minute advice?" Grace murmured.

"Lie with confidence. Tell the truth with flair."

"Reassuring."

* * *

A panel of five Bureau representatives materialised.

All wore identical robes — beige, soul-crushing, embroidered with little passive-aggressive runes like "please resubmit."

At the centre stood Agent Ferrow again, stiffer than ever, his moustache bristling with judgement.

"Grace Harper," he began. "You are here for final approval of Companion Bond #1478."

"Yes."

"Have you, at any point, participated in or supported unauthorised magical affiliations, rogue archivist interactions, or knowledge-unsealing rituals?"

"Define 'participate'," she said brightly.

Ferrow ignored that. "Do you believe your companion represents a threat?"

Grace looked at Leo. "Only to poorly stored pastries."

Leo flicked his tail. "Guilty."

* * *

Suddenly, the chamber lights dimmed.

A resonance began to build — low, vibrating magic pulsing like a heartbeat.

The scrolls on the panel's table began to glow. One of them — Leo's original registration parchment — burst into violet flame.

Ferrow shouted, "Contain it!"

Too late.

Leo doubled over, tail lashing, eyes wide.

A burst of memory-saturated magic exploded from his chest, projecting visions across the chamber like a broken film reel:

- A girl with ash-blonde hair whispering goodbye.
- Leo clutching a shattered rune.

- A shadow with no name, curling through the cracks of Claremont.
- Grace — asleep in her flat — a faint echo of that girl, but *not* her.

*　*　*

Everyone froze.

Grace took a step forward.

Leo gasped, "They *know* now."

Ferrow raised a hand. "You are harboring Claremont residue. You are unstable. The bond is compromised."

Grace shouted, "He's *not* dangerous—!"

But Ferrow spoke a sealing phrase: "Bureau Override. Section 9. Anchor nullification protocol engaged."

Ropes of spectral light shot toward Grace.

Leo leapt in front of her.

For a terrifying moment, everything was silent.

Then the ropes shattered — not from strength, but from resonance.

The bond between Grace and Leo flared gold — forged by chaos, stubbornness, and exactly three poorly written recommendation letters.

* * *

The hall shook.

From above, a sigil burst into bloom — not Bureau-made, but older, deeper.

Oberon's voice echoed from the sigil:

"She is claimed. The anchor holds. Back off, pencil-pushers."

Ferrow's eyes widened. "You involved the Watchers?!"

Grace grinned. "Turns out bureaucratic trauma makes great motivation."

* * *

Aftermath

An hour later, Grace and Leo sat on the back steps of the Bureau's emergency garden — a calming area filled with enchanted daisies that whispered affirmations like "you're doing your best."

Leo was curled in her lap, purring slightly louder than necessary.

"They didn't nullify us," she murmured.

"Yet," Leo said. "They're still filing complaints in seven dimensions."

"They can file all they like."

He opened one eye. "You're not afraid anymore."

"No," she said. "Because you're not just memory. You're *here*. With me."

He blinked slowly. "I think I like this timeline."

* * *

Final Interlude: The Orange Cat's Journal (Entry #17)

Letter Status:

√ Bureau-approved

√ Emotionally risky

√ Bureaucratically exhausting

Anchor:
– Resilient
– Connected
– Mine

Threat Level:
– Public: Stabilised
– Private: Growing

Conclusion:

– Three letters. One bond. A future neither of us expected.

– The Bureau sees only files. She saw *me*.

Chapter Four: The Art of Standing Still

Part 1

The World Does Not Resume

The first thing Grace did after the Bureau hearing was go home, throw off her boots, and refuse to speak to anyone who wasn't at least 30% cat.

Leo approved of this boundary.

For a full twelve hours, they said nothing.

He curled up on her keyboard like a proper gremlin, and she sat on the couch, staring into the middle distance like a woman who'd just emotionally power-washed her soul.

London outside carried on as if a magical Bureau hadn't just tried to nullify her like an overdue library card.

The buses still honked. The rain still misted. Her upstairs neighbours still practiced interpretive plumbing at 3am.

But Grace no longer fit into that rhythm. It was like wearing shoes that remembered a different foot.

"So," she said finally, "what now?"

Leo, eyes still closed, yawned. "We stand still."

Grace blinked. "That's the plan?"

"We don't move. We don't apply. We don't volunteer for magical errands or interdimensional poker tournaments. We let the chaos go around us. For once."

Grace frowned. "That's not very protagonist of us."

"That's why it'll work."

* * *

Part 2

An Attempt at Normal Is Doomed from the Start

On Monday, Grace brushed her hair, ironed her shirt, and opened her laptop to find a job.

Not a magical job.

Not an "interdimensional bond enforcement officer" role.

Just something normal.

Data entry. Customer service. Filing things alphabetically in rooms that didn't breathe.

She updated her CV. Left off the words "summoned by Bureau" and "defended my sentient orange cat in a trial of magical sincerity."

She did, however, include her experience managing stakeholder expectations and "complex filing systems under pressure."

Leo called that "the polite version of lying."

Grace replied, "It's called resume translation. Look it up."

* * *

She applied for three roles before lunch.

- One was in logistics.
- One involved a suspicious amount of spreadsheets.
- One was at a bookstore that promised a "cozy environment" and "minimum goat-related interruptions," which frankly raised more questions than it answered.

Afterwards, she went for a walk.

Leo, of course, came along, perched on her shoulder like a smug scarf.

"Do we *look* normal?" she asked.

"Absolutely not," he said. "But at least we look well-adjusted."

They walked through Camden. London bustled around them. No one noticed the cat with glowing eyes. Or if they did, they looked away politely — as Londoners do with ghosts, jazz buskers, and minor time anomalies.

* * *

They stopped at a café with outdoor tables.

Grace ordered a black coffee and a croissant that crumbled like a midlife crisis.

Leo ordered nothing and stared at the sparrows like a Victorian general assessing enemy troops.

A woman at the next table turned to them.

"Oh, what a *darling* cat!" she gushed. "Is he trained?"

Grace opened her mouth to say something neutral.

Leo interrupted: "I'm mostly self-taught, madam."

The woman screamed, flung her matcha latte in the air, and fled.

Leo licked a paw. "I regret nothing."

* * *

After the latte incident, they wandered into a second-hand bookshop that smelled like patience and marginalia.

Grace ran her fingers along the spines.

Leo hopped onto a shelf and knocked over a small ceramic unicorn.

The owner — an elderly woman wearing seven shawls and at least one small owl — smiled.

"I see you've brought your familiar."

Grace froze. "Excuse me?"

"Don't worry," the woman said. "He's got a look about him. And he didn't eat the unicorn. That's better than some."

Leo looked smug.

Grace bought a book on nonviolent conflict resolution and two used cookbooks she would probably never read.

* * *

Later That Night

Grace returned home feeling slightly more human.

She even cooked.

Leo sat on the windowsill, watching her stir something that could theoretically become risotto.

"You're adapting," he said.

"I'm trying."

He tilted his head. "Why?"

She paused.

"Because if I pretend hard enough, maybe the world pretends with me."

He nodded.

Then, quietly: "There's power in standing still. But sometimes... stillness is just the breath before the storm."

Grace didn't like the way he said that.

The lights flickered.

Somewhere in the hallway, a rune clicked into place.

And a shadow moved where no shadow should.

* * *

Part 3

The Stranger on the Staircase

The next morning, Grace opened her front door and nearly tripped over a basket.

It was wicker, lined with gingham, and radiated the unmistakable aura of Someone Who Tries Too Hard.

Inside sat a jar of homemade jam, two oat biscuits, and a handwritten note in elegant, looping cursive:

"Welcome to our building. Please enjoy these tokens of neighbourly harmony.
I do hope your cat isn't emotionally unstable.
Warmest regards,
Miss Peregrine — Flat 4D."

Grace narrowed her eyes.

Leo leapt onto the basket and peered at the note.

"She thinks I'm unstable?"

"You literally talked to a latte woman and nearly started an interdimensional panic."

"She screamed too easily. I did her a favour."

Grace sighed. "Let's at least pretend to be civil."

Leo squinted toward the upper floors. "You can pretend. I have plans."

* * *

The Mysterious Miss Peregrine

That afternoon, Grace took the basket up to Flat 4D.

The door was painted forest green. Brass numbers. Immaculately symmetrical succulents on either side.

Before Grace could knock, the door opened.

Miss Peregrine stood there, tall and slender, dressed in a robe that might have once belonged to a Victorian opera ghost. Her silver hair coiled like elegant vines, and her eyes — slate-grey — assessed Grace like a headmaster with a particularly promising new student.

"Ah," she said, "the one with the... companion."

Grace cleared her throat. "Yes, about that. Thank you for the basket."

Miss Peregrine waved her hand dismissively. "Neighbourhood obligations. I didn't realise Bureau pairs were being placed here now."

"We're not *placed*," Grace said. "We're... unofficial."

"Unlicensed?"

"Temporarily sanctioned."

Miss Peregrine smiled. "Charming euphemism. Do come in."

* * *

The flat was a library pretending to be a lounge.

Bookshelves covered every wall, interrupted only by odd trinkets: a tiny hourglass spinning on its own axis, a bonsai tree whispering motivational phrases in Latin, a birdcage housing what appeared to be a single floating feather.

Grace sat cautiously in a wingback chair.

Miss Peregrine handed her tea. No sugar, but somehow already sweet.

"Your companion," she said, "is not just bonded. He's leaking."

"Excuse me?"

"Power. Memory. Residue. I can feel it in the walls."

Grace said nothing.

Miss Peregrine studied her. "You don't know what you are yet, do you?"

Grace set her tea down. "I'm a person. Who likes cats. And is very tired of mystical foreshadowing."

* * *

Miss Peregrine chuckled.

"Very well. But when the *other one* arrives, remember this: you were warned."

Grace blinked. "Other one?"

But Miss Peregrine was already standing, leading her politely to the door.

"One last thing," she said, "before you go."

Grace turned.

Miss Peregrine held up a small metal tag. It shimmered faintly.

"Do *not* let anyone give Leo one of these. Especially if they smile when they do it."

* * *

Back at Home

Leo was sunbathing on the windowsill when Grace returned.

She tossed the jam jar onto the counter.

"New neighbour says you're leaking."

Leo opened one eye. "Tell her she's projecting."

Grace dropped onto the sofa. "She also said there's another one coming."

Leo sat up. "Another what?"

"She didn't specify. But she said not to take shiny tags from smiling people."

Leo stared out the window.

"That's very specific Bureau assassination code."

Grace groaned. "Of course it is."

* * *

Interlude: The Orange Cat's Journal (Entry #18)

Status:
– Peace: Short-lived
– Risotto: Acceptable
– Miss Peregrine: Too perceptive

Anchor:
– Still pretending to be normal
– Still watching
– Still mine

Prediction:
– The new arrival is already here
– They're watching us
– I hope they brought snacks

* * *

Part 4

The Other One

Two days later, the Other One arrived.

Not with explosions. Not with shadowy cloaks. Not even with a dramatic fog machine.

He just... moved in.

Flat 3F.

Same floor as Grace.

Grace met him by the mailboxes.

He was tall, calm, and looked like the human embodiment of a lukewarm espresso — elegant, aloof, and not to everyone's taste.

He wore black. Carried a book titled "Temporal Ethics for the Aspiring Manipulator."

And — crucially — he was followed by a long-haired Siamese cat that walked with the casual menace of royalty.

The cat stared directly at Leo, who was observing from Grace's bag.

Leo hissed. Quietly. Offensively.

* * *

Grace cleared her throat. "New to the building?"

The man looked at her like she was an interview question. "Yes."

"I'm Grace."

"I know."

Pause.

"I'm Elias."

More pause.

"This is Sorrel," he added, gesturing to the Siamese.

The cat didn't meow. She *nodded*.

Leo muttered, "Oh, she's one of *those*."

Grace smiled tightly. "Nice to meet you."

Elias didn't smile at all. "You've made ripples."

She blinked. "Excuse me?"

"Bureau agents talk. So do Watchers."

Leo growled softly. "He's listening where he shouldn't."

Elias tilted his head. "And you're not hiding nearly as well as you think."

Grace didn't flinch. "Are you here for me?"

"No. I'm here for what's waking up."

* * *

Unwelcome Guests and Undeniable Signals

That night, the pipes groaned like they were remembering something painful.

Grace tried to sleep.

Leo paced the kitchen counters like a paranoid sentry.

"Do you know him?" she asked.

Leo stopped. "Not directly. But Sorrel? She used to work for the Third Circle. They specialised in memory extraction and containment. Dangerous stuff. Experimental."

Grace sat up. "Like Claremont?"

Leo nodded. "Only messier."

They both went quiet.

Down the hall, a kettle shrieked from an unattended stove. Except no one in Flat 3F had cooked anything.

* * *

The next morning, Miss Peregrine knocked.

She wore an expression that suggested she'd already had a premonition, a prophecy, and a very disappointing breakfast.

She didn't ask permission before stepping inside.

"Elias is not stable," she said. "And Sorrel is worse."

Leo scowled. "We figured."

"They're not here by accident. That building isn't on the Bureau's list anymore — hasn't been for six years. The shielding wards were deactivated."

Grace frowned. "So they're here for... what? Us?"

Miss Peregrine didn't blink. "They're here to finish what Claremont started. Or un-finish it."

She dropped something onto the table — a paperclip.

Except it shimmered.

Like it was holding something together.

"Keep this on you. It'll slow them down. If they try anything."

Grace picked it up.

It hummed.

So did Leo.

* * *

Interlude: The Orange Cat's Journal (Entry #19)

Threat Level:
– Elias: Moderate
– Sorrel: High
– Miss Peregrine's paperclips: Untested

Anchor Status:
– Listening
– Processing
– Still drinking too much tea

My Mood:
– Curious
– Protective
– Slightly jealous of fancy cats with better fur volume

Action Plan:
– Watch them

– Trust no one

– Sleep with one eye open (and one paw on the paperclip)

* * *

Part 5

The Echo in the Dream

That night, Grace dreamt of bells.

They rang not like instruments, but like warnings — low, metallic, vibrating through bone and thought alike.

She stood in the middle of the Claremont Courtyard — except it was burned, cracked, and dripping with something not quite memory and not quite magic.

In front of her stood the girl.

The same one from Leo's fragmented memories. Grey-blonde hair. Burned coat. Empty eyes.

She opened her mouth, but her voice didn't come out.

Instead, Grace heard her own voice echo:

"You're not supposed to be here yet."

Behind her, shadows shifted.

A circle of cats. Dozens. All silent.

All watching.

Then one stepped forward.

A Siamese.

Sorrel.

Her eyes glowed silver as she spoke directly into Grace's head:

"You're standing still while the timeline devours itself."
"Your bond is a liability."
"You're not her — and pretending to be won't save you."

Grace woke up screaming.

* * *

Leo jumped onto the bed instantly.

"Talk to me."

She gasped. "Sorrel. She—she was in my dream."

Leo's ears flattened. "That shouldn't be possible."

"She *talked*. Said I'm not... someone. Said the bond is wrong."

Leo was silent for a long time.

Then: "She's trying to fracture you. They want the bond to collapse on its own."

Grace wrapped herself in her blanket like a logic burrito. "It's working."

* * *

Elias Knocks

At precisely 8:08am, Elias knocked.

He wore the same black coat.

He held two coffee cups and a very calm expression.

Grace opened the door, pillow-faced and unamused.

"Peace offering," he said, holding out a cup.

She took it suspiciously. "Is this poisoned?"

"No. It's from the café on Wren Street. Try the cardamom syrup."

Pause.

"Can we talk?"

Leo, perched on a nearby lamp, hissed.

Elias raised his hands. "Just talk."

Grace nodded. "Five minutes."

They sat on the hallway steps. Sorrel lounged nearby, tail swishing like a silent metronome.

* * *

"I know what you are," Elias said, sipping his coffee.

Grace raised an eyebrow. "Care to enlighten me? Because I've got theories ranging from 'magical administrative mistake' to 'reincarnated mythological filing clerk.'"

"You're a mirror," Elias said. "Not a copy. Not a replacement. A stabilised echo."

Grace blinked.

"I don't speak cryptic until after breakfast."

Elias continued. "Someone once bonded to Leo. That girl. She died. But part of her anchored. Her essence imprinted. And something — someone — used that echo to hold him together."

"You think that's me?"

"I think it's *why* you."

* * *

Grace stared at him.

"I didn't ask for this."

"Neither did he," Elias replied.

Silence stretched.

Sorrel broke it with a single word, spoken aloud for the first time:

"Claremont."

It hit the air like a dropped stone.

Leo growled.

Elias stood. "We're going to trigger a memory cascade in three days. I'm inviting you to witness it."

Grace narrowed her eyes. "What's your angle?"

"To fix what's broken," he said simply. "Whether Leo survives it or not."

* * *

Interlude: The Orange Cat's Journal (Entry #20)

Dreamscape Breach:

√ Confirmed

Violation level: HIGH

Anchor Stability:

– 73% intact

– 19% confused

– 8% caffeine

Sorrel Threat:

– Dream intrusion

– Memory manipulation

– Probably judges your blanket

Elias Proposal:

– Memory cascade = dangerous

– Grace attending = worse

– But we can't afford not to

* * *

Part 6

Emotional Pre-Quakes and Pancakes

For the next two days, Leo malfunctioned.

Not dramatically — not in a "summon hellfire and punch time" kind of way — but in a smaller, weirder, infinitely more stressful sense.

It began with memory bleed.

He'd be in the middle of a sentence and swap tenses like a confused novelist:

"I told you not to—will tell you not to—*am* telling you not to put raisins in the pancakes, Grace."

Or he'd stop walking mid-step, eyes unfocused, tail twitching, and whisper things like:

"Too late for the fourth seal. She's already rewritten the coast."

Then shake his head and ask for tuna.

* * *

Grace tried to keep calm.

She made pancakes. She made tea. She re-read Bureau handbooks on magical instability.

She even called Miss Peregrine, who arrived carrying three quartz pendulums and a small, judgmental ferret in a scarf.

"This is normal," Miss Peregrine said, waving a pendulum above Leo's head.

Grace arched an eyebrow. "Normal?"

"For beings with fractured lifelines and traumatic anchoring incidents."

The ferret nodded solemnly.

Leo, for his part, was curled into a tight loaf, eyes half-glazed.

"He's *resonating*," Miss Peregrine continued. "Your bond is holding, but barely. If you attend this cascade, everything will either stabilise... or implode."

Grace sighed. "Lovely binary."

* * *

That night, Leo collapsed mid-jump between windowsills and lay twitching on the rug.

Grace dropped everything, rushed to his side.

His fur shimmered — not just in colour, but shape.

His form flickered: bigger, sleeker, feline and not, body half-formed between cat and something older, more abstract.

For a moment, he looked like an idea trying to remember how to be fur.

Then it passed.

He looked up at her, eyes scared.

"I don't know what I'm becoming."

Grace wrapped him in a towel and whispered, "Then we'll figure it out together."

He shivered. "You sound like her."

Grace didn't ask who "her" was.

Not yet.

* * *

Meanwhile, in Flat 3F

Elias sat in a lotus position, surrounded by spell markers and tiny brass mirrors.

Sorrel watched, unimpressed.

"She won't survive the cascade."

Elias didn't open his eyes. "Maybe."

"She's too bound."

"She's the only reason *he* hasn't unspooled."

Sorrel flicked her tail. "You're sentimental."

Elias opened one eye. "I'm precise. Big difference."

He reached into a drawer and pulled out a sealed scroll marked with the sigil of the Third Circle.

"Protocol Theta: Memory Collapse Contingency. Anchor Class Alpha."

Sorrel licked a paw. "You really think she's Alpha class?"

Elias smiled faintly. "She stood still while everything tried to move her. That's not just rare — it's *dangerous*."

* * *

Interlude: The Orange Cat's Journal (Entry #21)

Symptoms:
– Flickering form
– Temporal grammar disorder
– Tuna craving = unchanged

Anchor Response:
– Calm
– Protective
– Pancake-based therapy

Risk Forecast:
– Cascade Outcome: 52% Fusion, 36% Disintegration, 12% Bureau paperwork

Personal Note:
– I don't want to forget her
– But remembering hurts
– Maybe that's the point

*　*　*

Part 7

Two Choices, One Cat, and a Very Calm Betrayal

On the morning of the cascade, Grace didn't sleep in.

She dressed with intention: jeans that could withstand eldritch fallout, a sweater that said "Emotionally Available but Tired," and her Bureau-issued boots (which had somehow reappeared in her closet with a passive-aggressive note:

"In case of poor decisions.
— Management.")

Leo was already awake, grooming himself like nothing was wrong.

"You're calm," she said.

"I'm lying to myself impressively," he replied. "You should try it."

*　*　*

At 9:34am, the Watchers knocked.

Well — they didn't *knock*. They let the *concept* of knocking appear in her mind and then expected her to understand.

Grace opened the door to find Oberon standing there, hair slicked back, robe stitched with runes that rearranged themselves when you weren't looking.

They smelled like elderflower and deadline anxiety.

Leo bared his teeth. "You're early."

Oberon smiled. "You're late — to understand what this really is."

Grace crossed her arms. "I assume you're here to make an offer."

"Two," Oberon said, stepping inside. "One for each of you."

* * *

The Offer(s)

Oberon waved their hand.

Two chairs appeared, along with a clipboard and two glasses of water that judged you softly as you drank.

They sat.

Offer One: Grace enters the cascade, helps Leo retrieve the buried memory, risks losing her own identity in the process.

Offer Two: Leo is sealed temporarily. Memories frozen, resonance halted. No cascade. He lives — half-aware, half-cat, but "safe."

Leo growled. "You want to sedate me like an emotional grenade."

Oberon shrugged. "It's better than emotional shrapnel."

Grace stared at the water glass. "What happens if I enter and fail?"

"You become her. Or something worse. Something unfinished."

* * *

There was a long silence.

Then Leo spoke. "She's not ready."

Grace turned sharply. "Excuse me?"

"You don't have to do this."

Oberon raised an eyebrow. "How noble."

Grace stood. "I'm not letting them put you in stasis like a problematic USB drive."

Leo looked away. "You don't *owe* me this."

"I know."

She stepped closer, knelt beside him.

"I *choose* this."

Oberon nodded. "So be it."

They handed her a black key.

"When the room appears, turn it. And stand very, very still."

* * *

Countdown

That night, the building changed.

Grace and Leo stood in the hallway between Flats 3F and 4D.

Suddenly, a third door appeared.

Black wood. No number. Cold to the touch.

She held the key. It pulsed once.

"You ready?" she whispered.

Leo didn't answer.

She looked down.

He had shifted again — his fur twitching, his form warping subtly — not unstable, but vast. Like he was temporarily occupying *possibility* instead of mass.

He looked at her and said, in a voice layered with too many lives:

"Don't follow me unless you're willing to become part of the story."

She took a breath.

"Then I guess I'm ready to be fiction."

And she turned the key.

* * *

Interlude: The Orange Cat's Journal (Entry #22)

Options:
– Isolation
– Erosion
– Alignment

Anchor:
– Foolish
– Brave
– Mine

This Room:
– It remembers
– It writes back
– It will either end me, or name me

* * *

Part 8

The Cascade Chamber

When Grace stepped through the black door, the world folded.

Not in a violent, explosive way — but quietly. Like an envelope sealing itself, like a breath being held across space.

She stood on what might have been a floor made of light, or stone, or thought. Around her stretched a circular room with no ceiling and too many walls.

Each wall pulsed with a different version of herself:

- One in Bureau robes, frowning.
- One as a child, holding a plush fox.
- One asleep, curled in a library aisle.
- One whispering to Leo, but in a language Grace didn't know she spoke.

Leo floated beside her — not walking, not standing — existing.

"Welcome," he said. His voice echoed across versions.

Grace looked around. "This is inside you?"

"It's where I go when memory misbehaves."

A light pulsed. The room changed.

* * *

The Girl

She stood there.

The one from the dreams.

Grey-blonde hair. Worn coat. Scars like punctuation across her arms.

She smiled, and Grace felt something in her ribcage unlock.

"You've always been the echo," the girl said.

"I don't understand," Grace replied.

"You're not *me*. But the universe needed a pattern. Something familiar enough for him to survive."

Leo stepped forward. "She's not your copy."

"No," the girl said softly. "She's your *correction*."

* * *

The Cascade Begins

The walls began to rotate.

Each showed a moment — a flash of time pulled from Leo's lifeline:

- Claremont, before the collapse.
- A rooftop in another London, filled with orange tulips.
- A laboratory where cats walked upright and spoke in equations.
- The sealing — Leo holding a rune and screaming, "Not her. Not *her*—"

Grace staggered.

Each memory vibrated in her bones. Each moment she hadn't lived but *could* have.

Then came the final wall.

A blank one.

It pulsed gold.

Leo touched it.

"I never saw this one," he whispered.

It opened.

* * *

The Truth

Inside was not a memory — but a possibility.

A version of the world where Grace had never met Leo.

She worked in HR.

Drank too much tea.

Had a birthday she forgot every year.

Was *fine*.

But also a little… faded.

Leo looked at it and said, "Without you, I would've survived. But I wouldn't have healed."

Grace looked at it and said, "Without you, I wouldn't have started breaking in the right direction."

The memory shimmered.

Then dissolved.

In its place appeared a door.

On it:

"Bond Confirmed: Evolving."

* * *

Reconstruction

The cascade chamber began to dim.

Walls folded inward.

Versions collapsed into one.

Grace stood still — not frozen, but centered.

Leo stepped beside her. No longer glitching. No longer unsure.

He looked like himself. But more.

Whole.

"You anchored me," he said.

She smiled. "You *reminded* me."

The black door reappeared behind them.

Oberon stood beside it, clapping slowly.

"Touching," they said. "Truly. And incredibly dangerous."

Grace raised an eyebrow. "What, no 'well done'?"

"No," Oberon said. "But you can keep the key."

* * *

Interlude: The Orange Cat's Journal (Entry #23)

Cascade Result:

– Anchor: Reinforced

– Me: Stabilised

– Shadows: Stirring

New Risk:

– The timeline noticed us

– The Bureau won't sit still forever

– Neither will the Other One

Conclusion:

– We're not standing still anymore

– We're moving

– Together

* * *

Part 9

Identity Theft (But Make It Existential)

Grace stumbled out of the black door and into the hallway of her building like a cat thrown from a centrifuge. Everything looked the same, but sharper. Louder. As if the world had gotten an upgrade and no one had installed the patch notes.

Leo followed behind, tail high, steps steady.

"You're walking like a sentient proverb," she said, winded.

"Do I look enlightened?" he asked, smugly.

"You look smug."

"Close enough."

* * *

They barely made it to their flat before Elias was waiting.

Not inside.

Not knocking.

Just standing in the corridor like a magical audit.

"You opened it," he said. Not a question.

"Yes," Grace replied, "and no, I didn't break anything. Except maybe linear narrative."

He studied her with a gaze like a finely tuned MRI.

"You're different."

She leaned against the wall. "You noticed."

Leo said, "Her mind is more... co-authored now."

Elias narrowed his eyes. "Which version of you is driving?"

Grace blinked. "Excuse me?"

"There were echoes in that chamber. You *absorbed* some of them."

"I didn't ask for that!"

"Intent isn't the point. Stability is."

* * *

Before Grace could reply, Sorrel stepped out of the shadows.

Because of course she had shadows.

She sat delicately, looked up at Grace, and said, "We ran a test. You failed."

Grace stared. "I don't remember agreeing to a test."

"You didn't," Sorrel replied. "That was the test."

Leo hissed, but Grace held up a hand.

"What did I fail?"

"Singularity," Sorrel replied. "You were supposed to remain one self. Instead, you've become... composite."

"Meaning?"

"You're not *Grace Harper* anymore. Not fully. You're now Grace Harper 1.03b, with optional backstory DLC."

Leo muttered, "She's being poetic. You're fine."

Elias sighed. "You're not unstable. Yet. But the Bureau won't like this."

"They never do," Grace said. "They barely like their own reflection."

* * *

The Knock

An hour later, the Bureau knocked.

Properly this time.

Knock-knock-knock, followed by a polite, soul-deep magical pulse that said *We Are Watching You And Your Flat Smells Like Treason.*

Grace opened the door to find three agents standing there.

Agent Ferrow was back, moustache bristling like a tactical asset.

He held a clipboard that radiated contempt.

"Miss Harper," he said, "we've detected a Level Delta Resonance Event originating from this premises. Would you like to comment before we commence sanctions?"

Grace leaned on the doorframe. "Can I comment *after* I make tea?"

"No."

Leo slid between her legs. "She saved a life. Mine. That should count for something."

Ferrow scowled. "That depends on how long that life remains legally contained."

* * *

Containment or Recognition

They wanted her to come in for "voluntary resonance screening."

She said no.

They wanted to scan Leo.

He refused.

They threatened to revoke her anchor certification.

She threw the paperclip Miss Peregrine had given her into the air — it exploded in a brief burst of anti-bureaucratic deflection magic and singed Ferrow's moustache.

"Very well," he snapped, eyes watering. "But you are now formally listed as an *anomalous anchor under review*."

"Do I get a badge?" Grace asked sweetly.

"No," Ferrow snapped. "You get a countdown."

And then they left.

* * *

Grace turned to Leo. "Well?"

He looked up at her, fur still glowing faintly gold.

"We're no longer under the radar."

"Were we ever?"

"No," he said, and yawned. "But now we're marked."

* * *

Interlude: The Orange Cat's Journal (Entry #24)

Bureau Visit:
– Unpleasant
– Unimpressed
– Unshaved (Ferrow's moustache now 13% shorter)

Anchor Evolution:
– Grace 1.03b confirmed
– Stability: 82%
– Identity conflict: beginning

Prediction:
– The next move won't be ours
– The next chapter will not be quiet

* * *

Part 10

The Flat That Forgot Itself

Grace woke to silence.

Not the peaceful, bird-chirping kind.
The wrong kind.
The kind of silence that happens when something's missing.

She sat up and immediately noticed it.

Flat 3F was gone.

Not locked. Not empty.

Just… not there.

The hallway wall was seamless — smooth plaster, no door, no number, no sign it had ever been anything but wall.

Grace reached out, hand trembling.

Leo swatted her wrist midair. "Don't."

"Why not?"

"Because it might remember you."

* * *

Ghosting, Spatial Edition

Miss Peregrine arrived within twenty minutes, summoned by Leo's emergency candle — which he lit upside down, while muttering something about "planar courtesy."

She brought a satchel, a scrying monocle, and a flask that smelled like vengeance and lavender.

After peering through the monocle for exactly six seconds, she said:

"Well. Someone's used a forget-chamber seal."

"On the *flat?*" Grace said, incredulous.

"On the memory *of* the flat," Miss Peregrine corrected. "Only Level Five archivists or above have clearance to access that sort of spatial denial."

Leo paced. "This wasn't subtle. It's not a message. It's a warning."

Miss Peregrine agreed. "They're cleaning up loose variables. And Elias just became *very* loose."

* * *

Elias, Or What's Left

Grace tried calling.

His phone was "temporally disconnected."

She tried knocking on the wall.

It echoed.

She tried saying his name in three different magical dialects.

Nothing.

Sorrel, however, appeared.

In her usual smug, silent way — sitting on Grace's doorstep, tail swishing like a clock.

Grace opened the door. "Where is he?"

The cat blinked slowly, then whispered in a voice like static:

"He's in review."

Grace frowned. "Bureau?"

Sorrel shook her head. "Worse. The Watchers have their own court."

Leo growled. "Of course they do."

Grace folded her arms. "Why?"

Sorrel stood, stretched, and said simply:

"He remembered something he wasn't supposed to."

And then she vanished.

* * *

The Letter from the Anchor Registry

The envelope appeared under Grace's teacup.

Which was impressive, since she had not lifted the teacup all morning.

Inside was a single sheet:

ANCHOR REGISTRY NOTICE

Subject: Grace Harper (Designated Anchor, Class B)

Due to recent fluctuations in cognitive-liminal resonance and suspected non-linear echo integration, you are requested to attend a formal Anchor Assessment.

Date: 03:03am, next full moon
Location: Registry of Abstract Compliance, Subfloor 7, Bureau Central

Bring your bonded entity.

Bring snacks. (Optional but recommended.)

— R.A.C., Division 2

Grace read it twice.

Leo peeked at it, then muttered: "Bring snacks? What kind of eldritch nonsense etiquette is that?"

Grace sighed. "The charming kind."

* * *

Meanwhile, in a Dream

Leo stood in a corridor of doors.

He was not dreaming — not exactly.

It was more like remembering in a future tense.

Door One: Grace, laughing, holding a kitten made of golden thread.

Door Two: Claremont, burning, and a shadowed figure whispering, "It wasn't your fault — just your turn."

Door Three: Himself. Older. Bigger. Not cat. Not man. Something in between. Watching Grace sleep from afar, unwilling to get close.

Then came Door Zero.

It was locked.

It was leaking.

And from within, he heard a voice that sounded like his, but colder.

"She won't survive the re-alignment."

He woke up hissing, claws drawn, tangled in the bedsheet.

Grace stirred. "Bad dream?"

Leo didn't answer.

He was still listening.

Because the voice hadn't stopped.

* * *

Interlude: The Orange Cat's Journal (Entry #25)

Status Update:
— 3F: Erased
— Elias: Vanished
— Sorrel: Cryptic as ever

Anchor Registry Summons:
— Mandatory
— Possibly fatal
— Definitely a terrible time to run out of biscuits

Dream Intrusion:
– Voice match: 91% probability it's me
– But I've never said those words
– Yet.

* * *

Part 11

The Registry of Abstract Compliance

They arrived at the Registry through a postbox.

Yes, an actual postbox.

Red, cast-iron, Queen Victoria crest. Located halfway between a defunct noodle shop and a tattoo parlour advertising "Runes Done Right."

Grace dropped a paperclip into the slot, turned it clockwise, and whispered:

"Two for classification, one for answers."

The world blinked.

When it reopened its eyes, they were standing in a marble hall the size of a whisper.

Columns pulsed with ancient citations. The floor was tiled in rejected metaphors. And overhead, a floating ceiling projected live edits of every anchor's narrative integrity score.

Leo squinted. "Yours is at 87%."

Grace sniffed. "Not bad for someone who once called an eldritch prosecutor 'emotionally constipated'."

A voice echoed from nowhere and everywhere:

"Welcome to the Registry of Abstract Compliance. Please refrain from lying, dying, or accidentally triggering recursion loops while on the premises."

* * *

Registrar Mirth

Registrar Mirth appeared as a man made of lines.

Literal ones — as if someone had sketched him in biro, but forgot to fill him in.

He wore a tie.

It flickered between paisley and despair.

"Miss Harper," he said, voice dry as paper, "thank you for arriving on time. Punctuality is one of the top five predictors of successful anchorage."

"And the others?" Grace asked.

"Survival. Consent. Cake. And narrative cohesion."

Leo raised a paw. "Are you being sarcastic?"

"Yes."

* * *

The Test

They were led to a chamber with no walls and infinite doors.

Mirth waved a hand and three doors appeared:

- One labelled: *"Truth"*
- One labelled: *"Memory"*
- One blank

Grace frowned. "Classic."

Mirth nodded. "You may enter any. Or all. Or none. But you must bring back something only *you* would recognise."

Leo looked up at her. "How do we know which one to start with?"

Grace cracked her knuckles. "The way all proper protagonists do."

She walked into the blank door.

* * *

Inside the Blank

Inside was a kitchen.

Her old one. Student flat. Tiny. Mouldy.

There was toast burning. Rain outside. A cat she didn't recognise curled on the windowsill.

Her younger self was humming.

Then she looked up.

"I almost forgot this," the younger Grace said. "It's where we first learned how to be alone without feeling lonely."

Leo padded forward. "I don't remember this."

"You weren't there," she replied. "But the space was shaped so you *could* be."

She picked up a chipped mug.

It read: "Emotionally Overwhelmed, But Polite."

She smiled. "I'll take this."

*　*　*

The Return

Mirth was waiting.

He looked at the mug. Nodded.

"Pass."

Leo sniffed the air. "That's it?"

Grace tilted her head. "Wasn't there supposed to be some kind of moral reckoning?"

Mirth handed her a clipboard. "We've done the math. You're still Grace. Complicated, composite, emotionally reorganised — but Grace."

He handed Leo a tiny paper crown.

"Also, your cat is now legally classified as a Sentient Companion Entity with Limited Reality Shaping Rights. Class F."

Leo purred.

Grace raised an eyebrow. "F for what?"

"Feline," Mirth replied.

***

Before They Leave

As they turned to go, Mirth stopped them.

"One last thing."

He handed Grace an envelope sealed with wax and dread.

"Open this only if he forgets your name."

She froze.

"What's in it?"

Mirth smiled. "The script."

Leo's ears twitched. "You mean *her* story?"

"No," Mirth said. "*Yours.* You just haven't finished writing it yet."

***

Interlude: The Orange Cat's Journal (Entry #26)

Registry Outcome:
— Status: Cleared
— Crown: Secured
— Mug: Questionable taste

Registrar Mirth:

– Untrustworthy

– Amusing

– Gave me a cat tax exemption form

Next Threat Level:

– Unknown

– But coming

– And probably shaped like memory

* * *

Part 12

The Standing Still That Wasn't

They returned home at 3:03 a.m.

Grace collapsed on the couch. Leo flopped across her legs like a bag of warm spells.

The flat felt normal.

But "normal" was already a lie.

* * *

An Envelope Opens Itself

The wax-sealed envelope they received from Registrar Mirth hadn't moved in the hour since they returned.

Now, without wind or hand, it peeled itself open and spat its contents onto the coffee table.

Three items slid out:

1. A photo: Grace at age twelve, with a cat she didn't remember owning.
2. A map: Torn, burned, marked "Claremont District Archive (Prohibited)."
3. A note, handwritten in familiar biro:

"The script has already begun editing itself.
If you don't claim authorship, someone else will."

Leo stared at the photo.

"That cat..."

Grace looked closer. It had Leo's eyes.

* * *

Glitching Reality

That morning, time skipped.

They made tea at 9:02 a.m.

At 9:04 a.m., the kettle had boiled — *twice* — but there was only one cup.

At 9:07 a.m., Grace had no memory of brushing her teeth — but her toothbrush was wet and minty.

At 9:13 a.m., Leo said, "Don't look outside."

She did.

And saw herself.

Walking toward the building.

Holding the same envelope.

Wearing the same clothes.

But her expression was blank — a face in screensaver mode.

Leo pulled her away from the window.

"It's a copy," he said. "Timeline residue."

"What is it doing?"

"Testing access. Seeing if you'll let it *replace* you."

* * *

Confrontation

That night, Grace found the second version of herself standing in the hallway.

No expression.

No shadow.

Just stillness.

"Who sent you?" Grace demanded.

The copy blinked.

"This is a courtesy visit. You've drifted."

"I'm real," Grace said.

"So am I," the copy replied.

Leo hissed. "You're an unanchored projection. Leave or I *unbind you*."

The copy looked at him — and for a moment, her face twitched.

Recognition. Pain. Remorse.

And then she vanished.

* * *

Claremont Reawakened

The next morning, Grace unfolded the map.

It shifted as she looked at it — roads she didn't know folding inward, names rearranging themselves like dream logic.

At the centre: a building marked "C.R.A.T."

Leo peered at it. "Claremont Resonance Adjustment Terminal."

"That's not on any official list," Grace said.

"It *was*," Leo replied. "Before the collapse."

Below the name, someone had scrawled:

"ENTRY DENIED
Unless standing still no longer applies."

Grace looked up. "What do you think it means?"

Leo tilted his head. "Maybe standing still was never the point."

* * *

Decision

The flat was quiet again.

But it wasn't peaceful.

Miss Peregrine sent a brief message by owl:

"You've been seen. The Other Echo is in motion.
Be careful what versions of yourself you leave unattended."

Grace tucked the map into her coat.

Leo jumped onto her shoulder.

"I think," she said, "we've done enough sitting still."

He purred. "About time."

And together, they stepped into the morning that already remembered them — and was waiting for an update.

*　*　*

Final Interlude: The Orange Cat's Journal (Entry #27)

Current Location:
— Reality-adjacent
— Memory-prone
— Tea-deprived

Grace's Status:
— Unstable

– Unyielding

– Unwritten

What I Know:

– We're not alone

– We're not safe

– We are, however, still incredibly stylish

Next Move:

– Rewrite the rules

– Reclaim the truth

– And if we have to bite a few timelines along the way... so be it.

Chapter Five: The Claremont Echo

Part 1

A Map, A Mug, and a Memory

They started with toast.

Not because toast would help decode a sentient map or fend off a rogue Bureau fragment—

But because Leo declared, "We can't chase ghosts on an empty stomach."

Grace accepted this with only mild suspicion. She added honey.

The map lay on the table between them, twitching like it had allergies.

"Any thoughts?" Grace asked.

Leo stared at it. "It's reactive. Paper made from archived event timelines. This thing remembers."

The map shuddered.

"Also possibly haunted."

* * *

Grace's Breakfast Breakdown

As Grace sipped her tea (which now insisted on being peppermint, even though she hadn't bought any), she made a list:

What I Know:

1. The Claremont Resonance Adjustment Terminal (C.R.A.T.) is real.
2. The Bureau deleted it from records.
3. Leo was once part of it. Maybe still is.
4. Something — someone — is rewriting versions of her.
5. Standing still was never safety. Just stalling.

What I Don't Know:

1. Why that cat in the photo has Leo's eyes.
2. Why the Other Grace cried before disappearing.
3. Why tea now brews itself if she stares at the kettle for 5 seconds.
4. Whether she's a person, a construct, or a very determined metaphor.

Leo padded over to her lap and purred.

"I think we should find C.R.A.T. before the Bureau does," he said.

"And if they already have?"

"Then we find what they missed."

* * *

The First Clue: Repeating Echoes

They didn't go far.

The first clue was two streets away — a café that Grace had walked past a dozen times but never entered.

Today, the door was unlocked, even though the "CLOSED" sign hadn't moved in a week.

They stepped inside.

It was empty. But not... abandoned.

The air shimmered faintly, like an unfinished spell.

And behind the counter stood a young woman with copper hair and no shadow.

"Welcome back," she said.

Grace frowned. "We've never met."

The woman smiled sadly. "Not in this version."

* * *

She handed them a mug.

Chipped. Blue. With a tiny cat paw embossed on the handle.

Grace stared. "This was in the flat. Back in uni. Before Leo. Before all this."

The woman nodded. "Time echoes strongest through things we forget we loved."

Leo sniffed it. "It's not enchanted."

"Not now," she replied. "But it remembers."

Then she handed Grace a folded note.

"Claremont isn't hidden. It's *displaced*.
Follow the map until it stops twitching.
Stand where your story should've ended."

Before Grace could ask her name, the woman stepped into the back room and disappeared.

* * *

The Map Stops Twitching

The map stopped moving at 3:34 p.m.

They stood in an empty car park where a Victorian archive building once stood — burned down in an unexplained fire a decade ago.

Now it was... nothing.

No weeds.

No bricks.

Just smooth, uncanny absence.

Grace stepped forward.

The air turned cold.

Leo's fur bristled. "This is where they contained the echoes."

"Meaning?"

"People like me. Versions of people like you. Collapsed timelines. Unstable memory nodes."

He looked up.

"And stories that were too dangerous to finish."

* * *

Interlude: The Orange Cat's Journal (Entry #28)

Day Status:
– Toast: Acquired
– Haunted mug: Collected
– Displacement site: Found

Mystery Levels:
– Identity Echoes: 85%
– Bureau Interference: Rising
– Coffee shop girl: Suspiciously poetic

Plan:
– Enter the nothing
– Recover the lost
– Don't die (ideally)

* * *

Part 2

The Hollow Archive

The first step into the absence wasn't like crossing a threshold.

It was like remembering a dream while still dreaming.

The air changed — tasted like ozone and old receipts. The sky thinned into static. Street sounds vanished.

And then Claremont was there.

Not fully.

But fractured — like a memory played on the wrong projector.

Half-built corridors blinked in and out. Desks floated sideways. Cats — or the idea of cats — flitted past like flickers of sentiment.

Grace reached out to touch a doorframe and her hand went *through*.

Leo bared his teeth. "This is a displaced resonance shell."

"English, please."

"It's a ghost. Of a building. Remembered hard enough to almost exist again."

* * *

The Memory Room

They walked through a corridor lined with floating file folders. None could be touched.

At the far end was a door marked "Internal Review: 10.14"

Leo growled low.

"That's the date," he said. "The day everything collapsed."

Grace pushed open the door.

Inside, chairs were arranged in a circle, surrounding an overhead projector showing... her.

A version of her.

Hair shorter. Coat different. Eyes... exhausted.

This Grace was talking to someone off-screen.

"We can't anchor him like this. The loop won't hold."

Another voice replied, one Grace didn't recognise:

"Then rewrite the anchor. Find another version. Anyone with compatible narrative weight."

And then the screen exploded into static.

* * *

The Delta Emerges

Behind them, a cough.

They turned.

And saw *him*.

Leo — or something like him.

Taller. Broader. No fur. No claws.

Just golden skin and slit eyes, dressed in a half-rotted Bureau robe.

"Version Delta," Leo whispered.

Grace blinked. "You *have* versions?"

The creature spoke. Its voice was velvet and thunder.

"You shouldn't be here."

Leo stepped forward. "Neither should you. You were deprecated."

Delta Leo's mouth curled. "Deprecated, but not erased. They archived me in the fallback layer."

Grace frowned. "What does that mean?"

Delta looked at her. "It means he replaced me. And now the loop's unraveling."

* * *

Confrontation

Leo narrowed his eyes. "You were unstable. Violent. You let her die."

"I tried to *remember* her," Delta snapped. "But you — you let them overwrite the memory with *this*."

He pointed at Grace.

"An echo. A patch note pretending to be a person."

Grace felt her fingers twitch.

Leo stood firm. "She's *real*. And she's mine."

For a moment, the two Leos shimmered — the resonance in the room buzzing like an overcharged beehive.

Delta backed away.

"You'll regret merging. The truth buried here will split you apart."

And then he vanished into static.

* * *

A Name on the Wall

Grace turned.

Behind the projector, something had changed.

A plaque. Bronze. Faintly glowing.

"Archive Room 12: G. Harper, Anchor-Class Candidate (Redacted)"

Grace stepped closer.

The plaque *responded*.

Her breath caught. Her chest ached.

The plaque now read:

"Grace Harper. Echo ID: 03.
Anchor Status: Provisional.
Role: Temporal Surrogate."

She touched the wall.

A spark leapt into her hand.

And she saw—

* * *

Flashback: The Anchor Chamber

Not a memory.

A truth.

She was on a table. Monitors buzzed. Cats — many, some human-like — stood in circles, speaking code and sorrow.

One voice rose:

"This one will hold. She's compatible. She *wants* to matter."

Then blackness.

* * *

Grace stumbled back.

Leo caught her. "What did you see?"

She exhaled. "My beginning. It wasn't birth. It was *selection*."

He looked grim. "You weren't chosen. You were *made*."

* * *

Interlude: The Orange Cat's Journal (Entry #29)

New Information:
– Claremont: Not gone, just displaced
– Delta Leo: Still glitching
– Grace: Definitely not a random girl

Emotional Status:
– Rage: 47%
– Existential dread: 63%
– Fondness for toast: 100%

Immediate Threats:
– Fragmented timelines
– Unstable selves
– Bureau silence (always loudest)

* * *

Part 3

Archive Room Twelve

The further they walked into the displaced building, the more unreal the air became.

Not dangerous — not yet — just uncooperative.

Shoelaces tied themselves wrong. Leo's fur wouldn't lie flat. Grace kept hearing a doorbell that didn't exist.

They arrived at Archive Room 12.

The door was open.

Inside were mirrors.

Dozens of them — hung floor to ceiling, leaning against bookshelves, mounted on chairs.

But none of them reflected Grace.

***

Failure Files

At the centre of the room stood a flickering console.

On it, a single glowing list:

ANCHOR CANDIDATE RECORD: GRACE

- 00: Rejected – non-reactive
- 01: Overloaded – terminated
- 02: Memory instability – collapsed
- 03: Current – partial success

Grace stared. "There were... others."

Leo stepped beside her. "You're Version 03."

She turned to him. "And you knew?"

He hesitated. "I suspected. But you're the only one who stayed."

They moved toward the mirrors.

One showed a younger Grace — angrier, louder, wreathed in static.

Another showed an older one — silent, eyes blank, body fading.

Each one stared back like an accusation.

* * *

The Whispering Wall

One mirror began to whisper.

"You shouldn't be here. You're not finished."

Grace leaned closer. "What does that mean?"

"You're not *you*. You're what they needed. Not what you were."

The glass rippled.

Leo swatted it.

It cracked — and the whispering stopped.

* * *

A panel lit up on the far wall.

A small screen blinked:

"Anchor 03 — system breach acknowledged.
Identity memory stream unlocked.
Ready to download fragment: 'First Incident.'"

Grace touched the screen.

A pulse hit her palm.

She dropped to her knees.

* * *

The Incident

She saw herself.

Running through a burning building — Claremont.

Holding a clipboard. Screaming someone's name.

Leo's name.

But it wasn't him.

It was a human. Tall. Gold-eyed. Laughing and bleeding and burning.

Grace screamed again.

Someone behind her said, "Leave him. He's already gone."

She refused.

Dragged his collapsing form through fire. Through memory. Through collapsing story logic.

Then—

Everything went white.

And she woke up in a bed.

In a flat she'd never seen before.

With a cat on her chest, purring like he'd always been there.

* * *

Back to the Now

Grace gasped and sat up.

Leo steadied her.

"I remember," she said. "I was a field tech. I broke protocol. I *saved* someone I wasn't supposed to."

Leo nodded. "They reset you. Anchored me to *this* version of you."

Grace clutched his paw. "But you're not just a cat, are you?"

Leo hesitated.

Then whispered:

"I was a person once. Maybe still am. But I chose to stay like this because... it's easier to hide when you're something soft."

* * *

The Mirror that Refused to Shatter

As they turned to leave, one mirror refused to let them pass.

It shimmered. Wobbled.

And then… stepped out.

Not a reflection.

A person.

Grace. But again, not.

This one had a scar down her left arm, a patch on her coat, and eyes that didn't blink.

"Version 02," Leo said.

The woman spoke.

"I'm not angry you replaced me," she said. "I'm angry they thought you'd do better."

Grace stepped forward. "I'm not trying to outdo you."

Version 02 smiled, grim. "Then don't fail. Like I did."

And she vanished.

* * *

Interlude: The Orange Cat's Journal (Entry #30)

Archive Room 12:
– Mirrors: Unnerving
– Grace clones: 2 for 4 unstable
– Console: Not user-friendly

Truths Confirmed:
– Grace = selected
– I = converted
– Claremont = erased to hide us

Unresolved:
– Why do I still remember the version of her who *never existed*?
– And why does it still hurt?

* * *

Part 4

The Conversion Room

The corridor beyond Archive Room 12 was wrong.

It looked ordinary — carpeted, fluorescent-lit, smelling faintly of lemon and resignation.

But Grace could feel it bending. Like the air had hinges. Like they were walking into a fold in someone else's idea.

Leo stopped at a black door with no handle. His ears flattened.

"This is where they did it," he said. "Where I stopped being… me."

Grace touched the door.

It opened inward.

* * *

A Room Without Gravity

Inside, nothing made sense.

Not just metaphorically — the laws of physics had clearly gone for tea and not come back.

Desks floated sideways.

Chairs hung from the ceiling like bats.

A single spotlight shone upward, illuminating a wide circle of floating glass panels.

Each showed a different image.

A Leo. Human.

Sometimes older. Sometimes younger. Always alone.

And always walking toward a decision.

* * *

The Central Pedestal

At the centre was a single console with one blinking prompt:

"CONVERSION LOG: SUBJECT L-117
VIEW MEMORY STREAM? [Y/N]"

Leo swallowed.

Grace looked at him. "Are you sure?"

He didn't answer.

He stepped forward and pressed **Y**.

* * *

The Memory: "Offer and Answer"

The room dimmed.

A projection began.

Leo — tall, exhausted, dressed in Bureau blue — sat in a chair facing a woman in gold-rimmed glasses.

She said,

"You can't hold the form. Your anchor failed. We need continuity, not sentiment."

He replied,

"Then give me a different anchor."

She frowned.

"None are compatible. Except the girl."

He hesitated.

"She's not ready."

"Then train her. From the start. But you'll need to change."

"How much?"

"Completely."

Leo stared at the floor.

Then whispered:

"If she remembers me... I'll go."

***

The Projection Ends

The console faded.

Leo sat down heavily on the floor.

"I made a bargain," he said. "They told me I'd die. That I wouldn't come back as myself. But if I could still protect her... I agreed."

Grace knelt beside him. "So they turned you into a cat?"

He gave a small, broken laugh. "No. *I* chose that form. I thought it would be... easier. To love her. To protect her. If I didn't remember what I lost."

She touched his face. "But you *do* remember."

He nodded. "Now I do."

***

A Scream From the Mirrors

Behind them, the wall cracked.

A voice howled — fragmented, high-pitched, and half digital.

Grace turned, and saw another her.

Taller. Pale. With black veins crawling across her skin like vines.

"Version 01," Leo said. "She broke protocol trying to escape her loop. She *remembered too much*."

Version 01's eyes glowed red. "You replaced me."

Grace stood up. "No. I *continued* you."

Version 01 screamed.

And charged.

* * *

The Shatterfight

Glass broke midair.

Panels flew like shuriken.

Leo leapt in front of Grace and yowled — his fur flaring with golden light.

Version 01 recoiled, hissing. "You were MINE!"

Grace stood. Hands trembling.

"I'm sorry they erased you. I'm sorry they buried your pain. But I'm not here to fix you."

Version 01 blinked.

"I'm here to carry you. Forward. Safely."

The broken version hesitated.

And then — for one terrible, beautiful moment — cried.

The vines faded.

She collapsed.

And shattered into light.

* * *

Something Left Behind

On the floor where Version 01 had vanished was a scrap of paper.

Grace picked it up.

It was a form.

ANCHOR PROJECT AUTHORIZATION — SIGNATORY

Subject: G. Harper (03)
Initiated by: L-117
Form: Voluntary Conversion

"The subject was chosen for her curiosity, resilience, and capacity to love lost things.
I will accompany her in whatever form necessary.
Even if she never knows who I was."

Leo stared at it.

Grace clutched his paw.

"I think," she whispered, "I always knew."

He buried his face in her coat.

And for the first time in both of their remembered lives, they didn't run.

They just stood still — not in fear, but in understanding.

* * *

Interlude: The Orange Cat's Journal (Entry #31)

Conversion Room:
– Memory: Recovered
– Truth: Not pleasant
– Grace: Braver than any anchor deserves to be

Version 01:
– Lost
– But not forgotten

Form Selection Regret:

— Cat body = fluffy

— Cat emotions = uncontained

— Cat sense of self = intact

I chose this. And I'd choose it again.

* * *

Part 5

The Library of Unwritten Things

The door to the Claremont Core Archive wasn't a door.

It was a pause.

A literal one — a frozen second hovering in midair, pulsing faintly like the heartbeat of a god caught mid-sneeze.

Leo squinted at it. "Temporal formatting gap. They didn't finish this hallway."

Grace poked the shimmering edge with her finger.

It felt like sticking her hand into déjà vu.

Then they stepped through.

* * *

Inside the Library

It was vast.

Endless.

Bookshelves arched in impossible spirals, each stacked with leather-bound volumes that changed titles when you blinked.

Floating cats — spectral and scholarly — wandered between shelves, nudging spines, whispering corrections, or sleeping in inverted gravity fields.

A massive sign hovered above the entrance:

"LIBRARY OF UNWRITTEN THINGS"
Curating truths erased for comfort since 1271.

Grace whispered, "What even *is* this place?"

Leo padded ahead. "The Bureau hides lies. This place keeps the truths that were too sharp to survive."

* * *

The Librarian

She emerged from behind a shelf of semi-invisible memoirs.

An older woman. Skin like paper. Glasses too big. Robe covered in quills that occasionally blinked.

"Welcome," she said. "Have you come to edit something, or to be edited?"

Leo stepped in front of Grace. "Neither. We're here for the Claremont records."

The Librarian sighed. "Everyone wants Claremont these days. It's fashionable again."

Grace held out the map fragment from her pocket. "We found this. It led us here."

The Librarian took it, squinted, nodded.

"You'll want the *Redacted Wing*. But mind the Echoflames. They get... enthusiastic."

*　*　*

The Redacted Wing

As they walked, books tried to jump into Grace's hands.

Some titles included:

- "The Time You Almost Remembered Being Someone Else"
- "A Complete History of All the Cats You Could've Loved"

- "Leo, Before Leo"

Leo growled. "Don't touch that one."

Grace smirked. "Jealous I'll fall for a better version of you?"

He rolled his eyes. "As if *that* guy would've made toast for you when you were hungover."

* * *

The Redacted Wing was darker.

The air shimmered like old film. The shelves hummed with suppressed truth.

At the far end was a single table with a file resting atop it.

Labelled:

"Anchor Project — Cat Integration Subprotocol 8A"

Leo stared.

Grace opened it.

* * *

The Truth of the Cat

Inside was a flowchart.

At the centre:

SUBJECT L-117
Chosen for high emotional resilience and adaptability to post-anthropic conversion.

Below that:

PROTECTIVE COVER: FELINE, ORANGE
Selected for optimal cuteness-to-threat ratio. Enables proximity without suspicion.
Public perception shielding: 96%. Bureau bypass rating: 82%.

Then:

ANCHOR PAIRING: G. HARPER (03)
Reason for match: Mutual loss potential.
Risk level: High.
Survival projection: Variable.

And finally, a handwritten note:

"He won't survive without her.
But she will only thrive if he forgets."

*　*　*

Grace sat down.

Hard.

"Was it ever real?" she whispered. "Us. This life."

Leo's voice was barely audible. "More real than the one they erased."

The Librarian returned, carrying a scroll.

"Someone left this for you."

Grace unrolled it.

* * *

A Message from an Unknown Hand

To Grace Harper

If you are reading this, then you've remembered too much.
That's dangerous. But necessary.

Claremont wasn't just a Bureau station.
It was a forge.

You and Leo are not accidents.
You're weapons.
But you chose peace.

That makes you dangerous.

Meet me where your memory hums.
Bring the cat.

— S.

Leo stared. "Who the hell is 'S'?"

Grace whispered, "I think... someone who still remembers us before we were edited."

* * *

Interlude: The Orange Cat's Journal (Entry #32)

Library Status:
— Haunted by truth
— Staffed by spectral scholars
— Shelves smell like regret and nutmeg

Findings:
— I'm adorable by *design*
— Grace and I are an emotional algorithm
— Apparently I *used* to be hot

Emotional Status:
— Tail puffed
— Dignity: wobbly
— Loyalty: absolute

* * *

Part 6

Where Memory Hums

They left the Library with a scroll, a headache, and a floating cat librarian shouting, "NO DOGS!" at no one in particular.

Grace held the scroll tight. It hummed in her hand, as if vibrating with forgotten names.

They took the Tube to South Clapham.

Then walked.

Down a narrow lane between a launderette and a Polish bakery.

To a building with no plaque, no number, and no shadow.

Grace had been here before.

But not as Grace 03.

Leo said nothing. But his tail twitched like a lie trying to hold its shape.

* * *

The Door Opens by Remembering

There was no doorknob.

Just a blank stretch of painted wood and an almost-sound, like a question that hadn't been asked yet.

Grace placed her hand on it.

Whispered: "I'm still me."

The door clicked open.

*　*　*

The Room That Shouldn't Be

Inside was a flat.

Identical to hers.

Down to the crook in the bookshelf, the mug with the chip, and the blanket that smelled like anxiety and chamomile.

Only... no one had lived here in years.

Dust floated like memories.

The air smelled of candlewax and endings.

And at the table sat a figure.

Human. Almost.

With silver hair and a coat woven from timelines.

"About time," the figure said. "Sit. Both of you."

* * *

Meet S

The figure poured tea.

It shimmered like television static and tasted like midnight.

"I go by S," they said. "I used to work at Claremont. Before it fractured."

Grace leaned forward. "How do you know us?"

S raised an eyebrow. "I don't know *you*. But I remember what *you're made from*."

They tapped Leo's head. "And I *built* him. Well. Helped."

Leo froze. "What?"

"You were going to unravel. You'd taken in too many false identities. Too much exposure to collapsing narrative structures. So we stored your memories in a *pet-shaped container*. Gave you someone to follow."

They looked at Grace. "Gave her someone to hold onto."

Grace asked, "And the cat registration rule?"

S chuckled. "That wasn't policy. It was a firewall. A clever one."

* * *

The Firewall Revelation

S stood and tapped the wall.

It rippled, revealing a blueprint.

PROJECT: CAT-SHIELD
Subtype: Bureau-Evasion Cognitive Mask
Authorisation: S | L-117 | Peregrine
Date: Before Collapse

"The 'registration' system," S explained, "wasn't for cats. It was for anomalies."

"Like Leo?"

"Exactly. If someone found him and *didn't* register him properly, the Bureau could wipe them both. But with three signatures from 'legitimate emotional anchors'? Bureau hands off."

Leo blinked. "That's why we needed the letters."

Grace muttered, "A bureaucratic forcefield made of friendship."

S grinned. "And cats. Don't forget the cats."

* * *

What's Coming

S's face grew dark.

"You've stirred the Echoes. Grace. Leo. Version 03."

Grace sat up. "Do they know?"

S nodded. "The Bureau will come. Not to erase. To absorb. They'll fold you back into the core program. Rewrite your parts. Use your bond as a weapon."

Leo's tail twitched. "What do we do?"

S pushed the scroll toward them. "Find the **Resonant Root**. It's your anchor's anchor. The point where your versions first intersected, before they were split."

Grace frowned. "Where is it?"

S smiled.

"That's the one place they *can't* erase."

* * *

Interlude: The Orange Cat's Journal (Entry #33)

Status:

– I was built?!

– I have a firewall?!

– I'm *literally* protected by paperwork and hugs?!

S:

– Possibly a wizard

– Definitely a smartass

– Probably used to be my therapist

Next Target:

– Resonant Root

– Location: unknown

– But I suspect it smells like toast

* * *

Part 7

The Resonant Root

The scroll from S didn't contain a map.

It contained a scent.

One Grace couldn't name but immediately recognised: warm bread, cracked earth after rain, and something else—like a hug you forgot you needed.

Leo sniffed it and sneezed. "That's... memory-grade olfactory encoding. Someone really didn't want coordinates written down."

"Can you track it?"

"I'm a cat. If I can't track smell, the universe is broken."

* * *

Finding the Root

They wandered South London's alleyways like dreamers on a scavenger hunt.

Until they found it.

A cracked garden gate in Brixton.

It led to nothing particularly magical: a concrete patch, two empty flower pots, and a deflated paddling pool full of leaves.

Grace stepped inside.

And the world wobbled.

* * *

Time Folds Like Laundry

Suddenly, it was sunny.

The paddling pool inflated.

The garden bloomed.

A younger Grace, no older than seven, sat cross-legged on a towel, feeding something under the bush.

Leo blinked.

It was a kitten.

Orange. Slightly too large ears. Tail twitching in rhythm with her heart.

"That's me," he said.

Grace crouched beside the memory.

Young Grace whispered, "Mum says you're not real."

The kitten curled closer to her hand.

She added, "But I'm going to keep you anyway."

And the memory faded.

* * *

The Root Reveals Itself

A tree grew.

Instantly.

Right where the bush had been.

It shimmered—part bark, part clockwork. Leaves whispered in overlapping voices.

Grace stepped close.

One word floated above it, projected like light through tears:

CONVERGENCE

Leo sat under it.

"This is where they pulled us from," he said. "From this moment. That bond."

Grace touched the bark.

And the tree opened.

* * *

Inside the Tree

They stepped into memory.

But not a linear one.

A spiralling, liquid-sense version of every "first meeting" they'd ever had:

- In a hallway of a flat neither of them remembered renting.
- In a Bureau lab, separated by glass.
- In a dream.
- On a train platform, both in the wrong year.
- In a classroom with no teacher, where Leo had paws and a nametag.

Each version fractured, mirrored, reassembled itself into one truth:

They had *always* found each other.
The *form* changed.
The *bond* never did.

* * *

The Conversation They Never Had

The tree's core was a quiet room.

A bench. A teacup. And two shadows.

Grace's voice whispered:

"If I break, will you still follow me?"

Leo's voice—human, soft—replied:

"Even if you forget how to ask."

Then:

"What if I forget *you*?"

"Then I'll wait. Until remembering feels like breathing again."

* * *

Grace looked at Leo.

"I don't remember saying that."

"You didn't," he said. "But you meant it. And I heard it. That was enough."

* * *

Exit Through the Beginning

When they stepped back into the garden, the tree was gone.

But a small wooden token lay on the towel.

Grace picked it up.

It read:

Anchor Verified
This version is real.

Signature: [L117]
Backup Code: [G03]

Leo purred. "That's our badge out."

Grace pocketed it.

And then the sky cracked.

Literally.

* * *

The Bureau Arrives

A black rift opened above the garden.

Three figures floated down—hooded, shimmered, Bureau-marked.

One spoke, voice flat as paper:

"Anchor has been located. Unauthorized convergence detected. Integration pending."

Leo hissed. "Nope."

Grace stood.

"No integration," she said. "This version holds."

The agent raised a hand.

Time froze.

Except for Grace and Leo.

Because they were already operating *outside* the rules.

*　*　*

Stand-Off

"You can't take us," Grace said.

"We're not your property," Leo added.

The agent's hood flared.

"You are constructs."

Grace stepped forward. "So are books. So are dreams. So is bureaucracy. Guess what survives longest?"

No reply.

Just a flicker of uncertainty.

Leo pounced—not physically, but narratively.

"We have a verified convergence. You *can't overwrite a locked root.*"

Silence.

Then—

The agents vanished.

The sky stitched itself shut.

The garden settled.

* * *

Interlude: The Orange Cat's Journal (Entry #34)

Root Found:
— Emotional level: catastrophic
— Dignity level: irrelevant

Scent Note:
— Toast. Always toast.

Status:
— Not just surviving
— Remembered
— Real

***

Part 8

The Grace That Wasn't

They didn't go back to the flat.

Too risky.

Instead, they followed the humming in the token to a pub that technically didn't exist anymore — condemned after a gin-related summoning incident in 1998.

The inside was untouched.

Dusty booths. Broken jukebox. One dart mid-flight for the past seventeen years.

Leo jumped on the counter and sneezed.

Grace slid into a booth and laid the token on the table.

It pulsed once.

Then again.

And then the mirror behind the bar changed.

Not their reflection.

Someone else.

* * *

The Face Behind the Glass

Grace recognised her own features.

But different.

Sharper eyes. No softness. The expression of someone who didn't *ask* for the world to explain itself — she dissected it and rewrote the footnotes.

The woman in the mirror smirked.

"Took you long enough."

Grace leaned forward. "Version 04?"

"That's what they call me. But I prefer my own name now."

Leo narrowed his eyes. "And that is?"

"Irrelevant. You won't remember it when I'm done."

* * *

Weaponised Doubt

The mirror rippled.

And Grace felt it.

Not physically — emotionally.

Like a tremor in her core. A whisper that maybe she *wasn't* the real one. That maybe the version from the tree, the memories, the bench—was all simulation.

Her chest tightened.

Leo yowled and leapt between her and the mirror.

"Don't listen," he snapped. "That's what she does."

Grace's hands trembled. "What is she?"

Leo said, "A countermeasure. The Bureau built her in case you ever *locked*. She's designed to unlock you from *yourself*."

* * *

The Mirror Fractures

Version 04 stepped through.

Not a hologram.

Not a ghost.

A physical version — with the same height, same voice, and just enough difference to be terrifying.

She circled the booth like a predator.

Grace stood.

"I'm not your enemy," she said.

Version 04 smiled.

"No. You're my *proof of concept*. The alpha test that somehow dodged the patch notes."

Leo hissed. "You're unstable. That's why they didn't deploy you."

She turned to him. "I'm not unstable. I'm *free*. I don't wait for someone to validate my reality. I *rewrite* it."

She touched the air.

And the pub began to... forget itself.

* * *

The Memory Collapse

The walls dimmed.

The jukebox stopped mid-fade.

The dart, finally landing, turned to dust.

Grace's token pulsed again—faster now, like a warning.

Version 04 spoke calmly.

"I'm not here to kill you. I'm here to show you you're *not enough*. That you're just a sketch. That if I speak the right sentence, everything you believe will unravel."

Leo roared—actual roar this time, all magic and rage.

"No," Grace said quietly.

The mirror-woman tilted her head. "No?"

Grace stepped forward. "You're not real."

Version 04 blinked. "Excuse me?"

"You're a backup plan. An emergency file. You think you're free, but you're a tool they forgot to delete."

And she pressed the token to her own chest.

* * *

Lock Override

A light erupted.

Not bright.

But *true*.

The pub sealed.

Not physically — but emotionally.

Time anchored.

Version 04 screamed.

Glass cracked.

The air reasserted itself.

The mirror shattered inward, swallowing her.

Her last words were:

"If I don't exist...
...why do I still *hurt?*"

Then silence.

And the smell of burnt toast.

***

A New File Appears

On the table, a new scrap of paper.

Not printed.

Typed. On an old Bureau machine.

Override Accepted.
Version 03 designated PRIMARY.
Counter-version sealed under emotional integrity clause.
Watcher status: pending.

Leo exhaled.

"Congratulations," he said. "You're now an official person."

Grace sat down, shaking.

"I didn't realise that was still in question."

Leo hopped up beside her.

"It always is. That's why it matters when you choose it yourself."

***

Interlude: The Orange Cat's Journal (Entry #35)

Pub Status:
– Technically illegal
– Now emotionally fortified
– Pint of ghost ale: undrinkable

Version 04:
– Disturbing
– Sad
– Still me, in a way

Grace:
– Solidified
– Stabilised
– Real enough to override a weaponized delusion

Honestly? I'm proud of her.

* * *

Part 9

The Choice of Shape

They left the ghost pub in silence.

The world outside felt more grounded than ever—like someone had quietly turned up the gravity just enough to make you feel your shoes.

Leo walked slower.

Grace noticed.

"You're thinking about it," she said.

He didn't deny it.

"They'll ask soon," he muttered. "The system's stabilised. They'll offer me the reset."

Grace paused mid-step. "The... reset?"

Leo looked up at her, eyes glinting.

"Option to return to human form. All memories restored. Full faculties. No more fur. No more hairballs. No more sneezing every time you use that lavender shampoo."

Grace's throat tightened. "And the catch?"

Leo didn't blink.

"You'd forget half of me. Everything after Claremont collapse. Maybe even the tree."

* * *

The Summons

They received it via pigeon.

An actual pigeon.

Wearing a lanyard.

It dropped a sealed envelope on their doorstep and gave Leo a sarcastic coo before vanishing into the fog.

Grace opened it.

Inside:

TO: L-117
FROM: SYSTEM RESTORATION CORE

Subject: Shape Reinstatement Offer
— Form: Original
— Memory: Reintegrated (with trade-offs)
— Risk: Medium
— Emotional Debt Transfer: 1

NOTE: Final approval requires emotional anchor (G. Harper) to witness simulation.
DO NOT IGNORE THIS LETTER.
FAILURE TO RESPOND WILL RESULT IN AUTO-CONSOLIDATION.

* * *

The Simulation Begins

It wasn't a room.

It was *every* room.

They stood in a version of Grace's flat—but it was cleaner. Brighter. The Grace inside wore office shoes. The Leo was... not there.

Instead, a man stood at her kitchen counter.

Tall. Familiar. Stirring tea.

Grace stared.

"That's you," she whispered.

Leo nodded. "Version of me. If I'd never changed."

The simulation-Grace laughed at something the man said.

Something she couldn't hear.

Leo glanced sideways. "This is the future where I said yes. Where I took the offer."

Grace swallowed. "Do I look happy?"

He hesitated.

"Yes."

***

Cracks in the Projection

But as they watched, the scene began to fracture.

The walls flickered.

The tea went cold too fast.

Sim-Grace blinked twice in the same second.

Leo frowned. "It's unstable. Because it's not *us*."

Grace turned to him. "Do you want this?"

Leo didn't answer.

The simulation began to collapse.

The system didn't like ambiguity.

***

Emergency Stabiliser

Another envelope appeared, this time in midair.

It read:

EMOTIONAL STABILISER REQUIRED.
CHOOSE ONE MEMORY TO BIND THE FORM.
ONE YOU BOTH REMEMBER.
AND WISH TO KEEP.

Grace thought.

Leo was silent.

And then she said, "Toast."

Leo blinked.

Grace added, "First morning. After I found you. I was late for work. You sat on the bread. Refused to move. I cried from stress. You licked my forehead."

Leo smiled. "I remember. You smelled like deadlines."

The system accepted the input.

And rejected the reset.

* * *

Reinstatement Denied

**REQUEST DENIED.
Selected anchor incompatible with reintegration.
Emotional persistence exceeds threshold.

FINAL STATUS:
FORM RETAINED
MEMORY PRESERVED
CONNECTION LOCKED**

Leo stretched.

"Well, guess I'm stuck like this."

Grace crouched and wrapped her arms around him.

"Good," she whispered. "You're *mine* in this form."

He purred.

"Always was."

* * *

Watcher Notification

A new message appeared.

Grace opened it.

TO: G. Harper (Anchor 03)
SUBJECT: Conditional Watcher Status

You have demonstrated emotional integrity under multiversal strain.
You retained selfhood under existential duress.
You remembered toast.

Congrats. You're officially confusing to the Bureau.

Welcome, Candidate.

— W.T.S.

Grace blinked.

Leo snorted. "Watcher Training System. You're in their weird alumni network now."

Grace smiled. "Do I get a hoodie?"

Leo's tail flicked. "Probably just paranoia and occasional hallucinations."

"Sounds about right."

* * *

Interlude: The Orange Cat's Journal (Entry #36)

Form Offer:
– Rejected
– Toast > Humanity

Watcher Grace:
– Official
– Emotional threat level: dangerously soft

Me:
— Still fuzzy
— Still Leo
— Still hers

Good decision. Would not trade fur for existential instability again.

* * *

Part 10

The Final Filing

Three days passed.

Grace went to work.

Leo pretended to sleep on her laptop while secretly browsing the Bureau's internal memos via tail-flick Morse code.

The scroll from S lay on the table, humming faintly.

Then one morning, a letter arrived—again, via pigeon, who this time refused to leave until bribed with half a croissant and an apology.

Grace opened it.

TO: G. HARPER
FROM: Office of Bureau-Civic Integration (Formerly Cat Registration Desk)

NOTICE OF FINAL INQUIRY

You are hereby summoned to attend a *formal verification hearing* regarding the permanent registration of your cat, known as LEO.

Hearing will take place at South Lambeth Council Annex C *(inconveniently behind the bin storage area)*

Attire: Semi-formal
Emotional stability: Highly recommended

Failure to appear will result in Leo being reclassified as a "sentient anomaly of domestic category" and subject to... complicated paperwork.

* * *

The Final Hearing

South Lambeth Council Annex C looked like a broom closet with delusions of grandeur.

A fold-out table.

Five chairs.

Three beings in judicial robes—only one of whom was human. The others were a tabby with a monocle and a shorthaired calico wearing AirPods.

Leo was seated on a tiny cushion labelled **"Petitioner."**

Grace sat beside him.

The lead judge—a woman who smelled of printer ink and disappointment—cleared her throat.

"Grace Harper. You have filed Form 9-A requesting official recognition of Leo as a feline citizen under Article 33-B, Sentient Attachments.
However, intelligence reports have raised concerns regarding his nature."

The tabby added, "He might be too *clever*. Also, he insulted my nephew."

Leo blinked slowly. "Your nephew is a literal sock with teeth."

"Still rude."

* * *

The Questioning

The judges asked:

- "Did Leo ever demonstrate knowledge beyond what a normal cat should know?"

"Yes," Grace replied. "He plays chess. Sort of."

- "Has Leo ever interfered with temporal protocols?"

"Yes. Once. But only to save toast."

- "Would you consider Leo your emotional anchor?"

Grace paused.

Then: "He's not my anchor. He's my *co-pilot*."

A hush fell over the room.

The calico paused her music.

* * *

The Final Option

The lead judge flipped the last page of the file.

"Miss Harper, due to the complexity of Leo's case, you are presented with two options:

1. Classify Leo as a feline citizen, with full cat rights and responsibilities.
2. Submit a new Form 9-E, reclassifying Leo as a 'Former Person in Emotional Containment Disguise,' to be converted into a human once more and added to civic records."

Leo turned to Grace.

"You get to decide."

* * *

The Decision

She looked at him.

All of him.

His orange fur.

His tail that twitched when she was anxious.

His eyes that had seen her through collapse, collapse, rebirth, bureaucracy, toast, mirrors, alternate selves, and pigeons with agendas.

She held up the pen.

And checked:

✓ Option 1: Feline Citizen

* * *

The Council Responds

The tabby sighed. "Very well. The cat is officially... a cat."

The calico meowed in agreement and fist-bumped Leo.

The lead judge handed Grace a certificate.

OFFICIAL FELINE CITIZENSHIP

Name: LEO
Species: Fluffy anomaly
Legal Status: Registered cat under interdimensional regulation 9-A
Emotional Function: Cooperative anchor unit
Status: Real. Registered. Remarkable.

Leo purred loudly.

"Does this mean I get to vote?" he asked.

The judge deadpanned. "Only in neighbourhood squirrel councils."

"Close enough."

* * *

Aftermath

They went home.

The certificate now framed in their flat, just above the kitchen sink.

Grace went back to work, but people noticed she smiled more.

Leo still refused to move off the toaster.

Their evenings became rituals of tea, cat treats, and unsolvable crossword puzzles.

But the air around them felt *anchored*.

Like the universe had finally accepted that their version of reality was... valid.

* * *

Final Interlude: The Orange Cat's Journal (Entry #37 – The Last One)

Status:
– Fully registered
– Publicly adored
– Occasionally mistaken for a fashion influencer

Grace:
– Happy
– Still making toast
– Still remembering

Me:
– I chose this form
– She chose *me*
– That's everything

Chapter Six: The Council of Complaints

* * *

Part 1

The Unexpected Committee Invitation

It began, as many unexpected bureaucratic horrors do, with a knock on the door and a cheerful liar holding a clipboard.

"Miss Grace Harper?"

"Yes," Grace said cautiously, one eye on Leo, who was currently licking marmite off her toast.

"Wonderful!" the woman beamed. "You've been nominated for civic participation in the Claremont Community Oversight and Grievance Suggestion Initiative Committee."

Grace blinked. "That sounds like... a lot of nouns."

"It is! It's also mandatory!"

Leo made a noise somewhere between a sneeze and a growl.

The woman handed over a folder.

"You'll be attending your first meeting tonight. Don't be late. Bring your emotional support mammal."

* * *

Part 2

The Hall of Mildly Agitated Democracy

The Claremont Community Centre was shaped like a shoebox, painted the colour of damp optimism. Its sign read:

NEIGHBOURHOOD OVERSIGHT HALL
"All complaints welcome. Petty grudges encouraged."

Inside, it smelled of tea, regret, and laminate flooring.

Rows of plastic chairs circled a long folding table where six people were already seated. Plus two cats. And a pigeon.

Grace entered with Leo perched on her shoulder like a pirate accessory who disapproved of everything.

"Welcome," said a man who looked like he'd been laminated himself sometime in the '70s. "Name?"

"Grace Harper."

He nodded. "Assigned seat: Row Two, between the Ornamental Hedges subcommittee and Feline Affairs."

Leo purred ominously. "I sense politics."

*　*　*

The Members

Grace sat.

To her left: a woman knitting what appeared to be a woollen traffic cone. "Ethel. Local hedge vigilante. Watch your hydrangeas."

To her right: a frowning man clutching a folder labelled *SQUIRRELS – CLASSIFIED*. "Trevor. Head of Rodent Threat Analysis."

Across the table sat a girl no older than twelve, sipping tea and reading *The Existential Risk of Modern Roundabouts*. She didn't look up.

"Watcher candidate," Leo whispered. "Low-rank, latent precog. Ignore the ribbon. She's dangerous."

Grace smiled nervously. The girl finally spoke.

"You smell like multiversal leftovers. I like it."

Leo hissed. "Told you."

*　*　*

The Meeting Begins

A bell was rung. Literally.

The laminated man, who introduced himself as Chair-Councillor Norris, opened a binder.

"Right. First item: The Sun."

A collective groan.

Ethel muttered, "It's too smug this week."

Trevor added, "Raised my electricity bill. Definitely conspiring with squirrels."

Grace raised a tentative hand. "Sorry. Are we... discussing banning the sun?"

The twelve-year-old precog shrugged. "Last week we voted to place it on probation. It ignored us. Rude."

* * *

Feline Affairs

Next agenda: Leo.

"Complaint received," Norris read, "from one 'Mrs Binchley, 14A', stating that the orange cat has exhibited... unusual charisma and possible mind control via purring."

Leo licked his paw, then made direct eye contact with the entire room.

They all simultaneously felt the urge to give him a treat.

"Motion to dismiss complaint," Grace said.

"Seconded," said the girl.

"Also," Grace added, "he's now a registered feline citizen."

Dead silence.

Trevor opened a different folder. "Is he licensed to attend committee meetings?"

Leo meowed once. Firmly.

Ethel gasped. "He invoked Clause 9-F!"

Norris sighed. "Fine. He gets a chair."

Leo jumped onto a folding chair and looked smug.

* * *

Unexpected Agenda Item: Interdimensional Surveillance Leak

As the room debated whether the local ice cream van had become sentient (verdict: "pending investigation"), the girl quietly passed Grace a note under the table.

It read:

"You're not here for hedges. You're here because your presence at the Root Tree was logged.
The Bureau is listening through the tea urn.
Don't look at it."

Grace very slowly did not look at the tea urn.

Leo whispered, "We need to leave. Now."

But then the lights dimmed.

And the next item appeared on the overhead projector.

It wasn't typed.

It was *etched*.

UNSCHEDULED ENTRY DETECTED: L-117 & G-03
SUBJECT: CONVERGENCE BREACH
REQUEST: OBSERVATION ESCALATION

Grace whispered, "I think the committee was the trap."

The girl nodded. "And you just triggered it."

* * *

Part 2

The Hall of Mildly Agitated Democracy

The Claremont Community Centre was shaped like a shoebox, painted the colour of damp optimism. Its sign read:

NEIGHBOURHOOD OVERSIGHT HALL
"All complaints welcome. Petty grudges encouraged."

Inside, it smelled of tea, regret, and laminate flooring.

Rows of plastic chairs circled a long folding table where six people were already seated. Plus two cats. And a pigeon.

Grace entered with Leo perched on her shoulder like a pirate accessory who disapproved of everything.

"Welcome," said a man who looked like he'd been laminated himself sometime in the '70s. "Name?"

"Grace Harper."

He nodded. "Assigned seat: Row Two, between the Ornamental Hedges subcommittee and Feline Affairs."

Leo purred ominously. "I sense politics."

* * *

The Members

Grace sat.

To her left: a woman knitting what appeared to be a woollen traffic cone. "Ethel. Local hedge vigilante. Watch your hydrangeas."

To her right: a frowning man clutching a folder labelled *SQUIRRELS – CLASSIFIED*. "Trevor. Head of Rodent Threat Analysis."

Across the table sat a girl no older than twelve, sipping tea and reading *The Existential Risk of Modern Roundabouts*. She didn't look up.

"Watcher candidate," Leo whispered. "Low-rank, latent precog. Ignore the ribbon. She's dangerous."

Grace smiled nervously. The girl finally spoke.

"You smell like multiversal leftovers. I like it."

Leo hissed. "Told you."

* * *

The Meeting Begins

A bell was rung. Literally.

The laminated man, who introduced himself as Chair-Councillor Norris, opened a binder.

"Right. First item: The Sun."

A collective groan.

Ethel muttered, "It's too smug this week."

Trevor added, "Raised my electricity bill. Definitely conspiring with squirrels."

Grace raised a tentative hand. "Sorry. Are we... discussing banning the sun?"

The twelve-year-old precog shrugged. "Last week we voted to place it on probation. It ignored us. Rude."

* * *

Feline Affairs

Next agenda: Leo.

"Complaint received," Norris read, "from one 'Mrs Binchley, 14A', stating that the orange cat has exhibited... unusual charisma and possible mind control via purring."

Leo licked his paw, then made direct eye contact with the entire room.

They all simultaneously felt the urge to give him a treat.

"Motion to dismiss complaint," Grace said.

"Seconded," said the girl.

"Also," Grace added, "he's now a registered feline citizen."

Dead silence.

Trevor opened a different folder. "Is he licensed to attend committee meetings?"

Leo meowed once. Firmly.

Ethel gasped. "He invoked Clause 9-F!"

Norris sighed. "Fine. He gets a chair."

Leo jumped onto a folding chair and looked smug.

* * *

Unexpected Agenda Item: Interdimensional Surveillance Leak

As the room debated whether the local ice cream van had become sentient (verdict: "pending investigation"), the girl quietly passed Grace a note under the table.

It read:

"You're not here for hedges. You're here because your presence at the Root Tree was logged.
The Bureau is listening through the tea urn.
Don't look at it."

Grace very slowly did not look at the tea urn.

Leo whispered, "We need to leave. Now."

But then the lights dimmed.

And the next item appeared on the overhead projector.

It wasn't typed.

It was *etched*.

UNSCHEDULED ENTRY DETECTED: L-117 & G-03
SUBJECT: CONVERGENCE BREACH
REQUEST: OBSERVATION ESCALATION

Grace whispered, "I think the committee was the trap."

The girl nodded. "And you just triggered it."

* * *

Part 3

The Chair Knows More Than Chairs Should

The room went still.

Not the peaceful kind of still.

The kind that happens when a room full of neighbours suddenly realises they've stopped being neighbours and started being assets in a containment strategy.

"Observation escalation?" Grace repeated, trying to keep her voice from sounding like it was reaching for the panic button.

The tea urn hissed ominously.

Chair-Councillor Norris cleared his throat, which sounded a little too much like booting up a legacy operating system.

"I move," he said slowly, "that we proceed with Protocol 11-C: Selective Reveal."

"Seconded," murmured the twelve-year-old.

Ethel whispered, "Finally. Been dying to see what happens when the protocols go off-script."

* * *

Selective Reveal

The projector flickered, then shut off.

The tea urn beeped.

And all at once, the fluorescent lights turned magenta.

Half the room vanished.

Not gone—just removed from Grace's perception, like a visual parenthesis.

Left behind were:

- The twelve-year-old girl, now glowing faintly and sipping tea from a cup that no longer had a bottom;
- Chair-Councillor Norris, who had unzipped his laminate outer layer to reveal a swirling lattice of translucent bureaucracy;
- And Ethel, whose knitting had turned into a constellation map, each stitch orbiting a glowing crochet hook.

Leo, very softly, swore in Feline High Tongue.

***

The Truth of the Council

Norris gestured at the now-dimmed table.

"We are the Claremont Sub-Cell of the Interdimensional Parity Commission."

Grace raised an eyebrow. "You're what now?"

Ethel waved her crochet hook in lazy spirals. "Reality needs oversight, dear. Even when it's disguised as community gardening complaints."

The girl nodded. "We monitor version bleed. Identity instability. Unauthorized timeline knitting."

"Knitting?" Grace asked.

Leo answered. "You've been walking through a reality held together by metaphor. They're the ones holding the needle."

Norris continued, "And your presence, Grace Harper, has pulled several old threads very tight."

He turned to Leo.

"And you, L-117, have reached Decision Threshold."

***

The Vote That Wasn't

"Hold on," Grace said. "What's being decided?"

The girl closed her book. "Whether Leo stays here—as is—or is... promoted."

Leo flicked an ear. "Promoted?"

"To what?" Grace asked.

Ethel replied, "To Watcher status. Permanent. Memory-anchored. Full awareness restored."

Grace frowned. "That doesn't sound bad."

"It isn't," said the girl. "Unless you like him this way."

Leo licked a paw nervously. "They mean I'll stop being a cat."

Silence.

Not just in the room—but in Grace's chest.

*　*　*

What It Means

Watcher Leo would remember all versions.

All timelines.

All missions.

He would become a cross-point—a living keystone of Claremont's broken map.

But he would no longer *be* this Leo.

Not quite.

Still him... but unbearably more.

Grace whispered, "Do *you* want that?"

Leo didn't answer.

He just looked at her.

Looked at the teacup.

The chair.

The certificate on the kitchen wall back home.

And said, very softly, "Not if it costs you the me you chose."

* * *

A Compromise

The girl raised her hand. "Motion to suspend the vote. Introduce Amendment 12-R."

Ethel nodded. "Part-time Watcher status?"

Norris's inner bureaucracy shuddered. "It's risky."

"Everything is," said Grace.

The tea urn hissed again.

Then printed a receipt.

It read:

Motion Passed:
Leo, Cat-Class Citizen, granted Provisional Observational Rank under Clause 9-Z.
Responsibilities: Minimal
Expectations: Vague
Fur Shedding: Unavoidable

Leo meowed.

Loudly.

Triumphantly.

***

Interlude: The Orange Cat's Journal (Entry #38)

Committee Outcome:

– Not demoted

– Not promoted

– Re-categorised as "Watchcat"

Perks:

– Still allowed on toast

– Can attend council meetings without paperwork

– Occasional visions

Downsides:

– Increased responsibility

– Cannot un-know what I now know

– Might be allergic to metaphors

***

Part 4

The Loophole Garden

After the vote, Ethel handed Grace a soggy envelope.

"This is your one-time pass to the Loophole Garden," she said, as if talking about a local allotment rather than a cross-dimensional anomaly. "Mind the fig tree. It lies."

Leo squinted at the envelope. "Is that written on lettuce?"

"It's legal if it composts," Ethel sniffed. "You'll want to enter before the next lunar paperwork cycle."

"Which is when?"

She pointed at a clock.

It was melting.

* * *

Entry Requirements

The envelope unfurled in Grace's hands, revealing not a ticket but a list.

Requirements for Entry to the Loophole Garden
– One registered citizen (species flexible)
– One cognitive dissonance event in the last 48 hours
– One memory you're not sure you had
– At least mild resentment toward a bureaucracy

Grace and Leo shared a look.

"Check," they said in unison.

The envelope turned into a door.

A literal door.

Standing upright in the middle of the community hall floor, framed by nothing but possibility.

Grace opened it.

* * *

Welcome to the Garden

They stepped into what appeared to be a garden designed by someone who had only seen photos of Earth gardens but was very confident in their interpretation.

Lawns were upside down.

Benches floated just above where you wanted to sit.

Fountains spouted ideas instead of water.

In the centre, a tree with purple bark and complaint forms hanging from its branches swayed ominously.

Leo sniffed. "I smell forgotten footnotes."

Grace nodded. "And... grape bubblegum?"

"That's the fig tree," Leo said darkly.

* * *

The Fig Tree Lies

It was enormous.

Its leaves shimmered in and out of relevance.

A sign beside it read:

FIG TREE – Category: Contradiction.
Do not trust it. Do not trust it. Do not trust it.

Grace asked, "Why bring me here?"

Ethel, who had appeared out of nowhere and was now trimming a topiary shaped like a gavel, said:

"Because the Bureau has overlooked you. That gives you power."

Leo twitched. "You mean she's an unregistered variable."

Ethel smiled. "Exactly. Her form was never fully logged. And you—well, you're a wildcard."

* * *

Clues Among Vines

Grace touched one of the complaint forms hanging from the tree.

It read:

"Complaint #447-B:
She wasn't supposed to retain that memory.
It was marked for deletion.

Re: Subject G. Harper
Date of Leak: 14th February
Related Entity: L117, form 'Li Li'"

Grace froze. "Li Li?"

Leo's tail stiffened. "That's not one of my known aliases."

Ethel said nothing.

Then another voice—dry, amused, nostalgic—drifted through the Garden like mist.

"Technically, it was mine."

* * *

Enter the Echo

He stood by the rosebushes that bloomed paradoxes.

Tall.

Wearing a black coat.

Cat ears twitched under his hood.

Leo stared. "No."

Grace whispered, "Is that...?"

"Yes," said the man. "You can call me Li Li. At least, here."

* * *

Interlude: The Orange Cat's Journal (Entry #39)

The Garden:
– Gravity optional

– Chronology discouraged

– Tree very smug

Li Li:
– Not me

– Not Grace's

– But connected

Things I Hate:
– Bureau paperwork

– Cats who look better in coats than I do

– Fig trees with opinions

* * *

Part 5

The Cat Who Could Have Been

The man in the coat walked like he wasn't used to the ground staying still. His movements were too smooth, like he'd been paused in time too long and still hadn't quite adjusted to the ungraceful art of walking again.

He extended a hand to Grace.

"Hello again," he said. "Or for the first time, depending on the version."

Grace didn't shake it.

"Who are you *really*?"

Li Li smiled, gently.

"I'm what Leo could've become—if he had taken the promotion."

Leo narrowed his eyes. "Impossible. I rejected full Watcher merge protocol."

"You did," Li Li nodded. "But the Bureau ran a clone fork based on your earlier behavioural dataset. I was the result."

Leo flicked his tail. "Then you're a... simulation?"

"A retired one. Relegated to the Loophole Garden after I started asking questions they couldn't answer. Turns out, even Bureau projections get existential dread."

* * *

The Blank in Grace

Li Li turned to Grace.

"You, however, are harder to categorise."

Grace folded her arms. "Because I wasn't supposed to remember the tree?"

"No. Because part of you never *loaded* properly."

He plucked a complaint form from the tree and handed it to her.

It read:

**FORM 42-J:
Memory node G-03 lacks standard emotional root signature. Correlation failure with designated pre-event memories.

Primary suspect: Entity J.**

"Entity J?" Grace asked.

Li Li nodded. "Codename for a now-erased construct. Last seen curled on your chest the night before the Claremont rupture."

Leo bristled. "Li Ju?"

Li Li sighed. "Yes. 'Li Ju' wasn't just a cat. He was the patch."

* * *

The Patch Theory

Li Li sat beside the fig tree, which fluttered disapprovingly.

"Claremont's last stable test run relied on two anchors: you and him. When it collapsed, the Bureau erased his formal record and tried to reboot you with Leo as the new guide. But…"

He pointed to Grace's chest.

"That space? The part of you that remembers things you never lived? That's him."

Leo whispered, "He never left. Just changed format."

Grace blinked.

"So I'm… carrying his memory?"

"More than that," Li Li said. "You're carrying his decision."

She frowned. "What decision?"

Li Li met her gaze.

"To love you enough to disappear."

* * *

The Garden Reacts

The ground trembled slightly.

Complaint forms began detaching from the tree, floating like confetti in a storm of realisation.

Grace's hands shook.

Leo pressed against her side, his purring now a low, steady frequency that pulsed comfort.

Li Li stood.

"You need to complete the record. The system still sees you as a partially rendered citizen."

Grace wiped her eyes. "How?"

Li Li handed her a final form. It was blank.

Except for:

Return to the first moment.
Do not observe. Participate.

***

The Door of Recall

Behind the fountain of unfiled appeals, a wooden gate appeared.

Simple.

Quiet.

Smelling of marmalade and dust.

"Step through," Li Li said. "You'll have five minutes. No talking. Just feel."

Leo whispered, "I'll stay here. In case things unravel."

Grace nodded.

Opened the door.

And vanished into her own forgotten beginning.

***

Interlude: The Orange Cat's Journal (Entry #40)

Li Li:
– Clone ghost

– Too poetic

– Might be my emotionally intelligent cousin

Grace:

– Contains multitudes

– Contains patches

– Contains *him*

Me:

– Still here

– Still her present

– But maybe not her only story

* * *

Part 6

The First Purring

Grace stepped through the wooden door and was instantly swallowed by stillness.

No wind.

No temperature.

No up.

No down.

And then—

Light.

Gentle, late-afternoon light poured through gauzy curtains. She stood—no, *was*—inside a familiar flat.

Her flat.

But not quite.

The walls had fewer books. The kettle was older. The clock hadn't been set correctly since Daylight Saving ended last year.

Grace knew where she was.

The day before Claremont cracked.
The day she found him.

* * *

The Memory Replays

The door opened.

A younger Grace—slightly more tired, slightly less sure—walked in carrying groceries and a box.

The box mewed.

Real Grace (now the observer) gasped.

From inside the box, a tiny, citrus-furred kitten poked his head out.

Not Leo.

Li Ju.

No strange intelligence in his eyes.

Just warmth.

And something impossibly kind.

The memory-Grace hesitated.

Then whispered, "You don't have a tag, huh?"

Li Ju purred.

Grace (the present one) felt her chest ache.

* * *

The Loop Closes

She knew what happened next.

She'd pour a bowl of cereal for herself, then use the same bowl for the cat because she hadn't unpacked the dishes.

She'd curl up on the sofa.

He'd crawl onto her chest and purr until she forgot to cry.

And that night, she would dream of a garden with a fig tree—

No. Not a dream. A message.

The memory paused.

Real Grace stepped forward.

Into herself.

For one moment—she felt it all again.

Not just the purring.

The decision.
That he was never meant to stay.
That his purpose was singular, brief, and beautiful.

✱ ✱ ✱

Confirmation

A voice—soft, mechanical, but warm—echoed through the frozen memory.

**EMOTIONAL RECORD RECOVERED
PATCH 3B: LOVE-THROUGH-LOSS

CONFIRM IDENTITY:
GRACE HARPER
SUBJECT: LI JU

Did it happen?

YES / NO**

Grace's hand hovered.

Trembled.

Then tapped:

✓ YES

The memory faded.

But not the feeling.

* * *

Return with Evidence
Grace stepped back into the Loophole Garden, dazed.
Leo was waiting.

In his paws: a small cassette recorder.
Old-fashioned.
Dusty.
Marked with a tiny sticker of an orange cat.

"I found this growing under the fig tree," he said.
"It started purring when you confirmed."

Grace took it.
Pressed play.

A low, warbling *miao* filled the air.
Then a layered feline hum—like a lullaby from somewhere warm.

Leo translated softly:

"If I can't stay long,
I'll be a sound you always remember.
Wherever you are,
The orange part of me will always nap in your heart."

* * *

The Garden Approves

The fig tree dropped one final complaint form.

But it wasn't a complaint.

It was a certificate.

EMOTIONAL LOOP RESOLVED

Subject: G-03 (Grace Harper)
Patch Acknowledged: Li Ju

Identity Status: Whole
Watcher Alignment: Confirmed

Congratulations. You are now emotionally real. Bureau is mildly horrified.

Ethel, knitting nearby, wiped a tear.

"You're one of us now, love. Full emotional permissions and all."

Leo added, "And fig tree seems to like you now. Probably."

* * *

Interlude: The Orange Cat's Journal (Entry #41)

Patch confirmed.
Cat remembered.
Self stable.

Grace has all her pieces now.

Me? I'm still a cat.
But now I share a heart with a memory that wasn't mine—
And that's okay.

It's getting crowded in here.

Emotionally, I mean.
Not litter-box-wise.

* * *

Part 7

The Version That Wouldn't Die

When Grace and Leo returned to the Council Hall, it was no longer just a broom closet with delusions of power.

It was *buzzing*.

The fluorescent lights blinked like they'd seen a ghost.

Ethel met them at the door with a teacup that emitted a low growl. "She's stirring."

Grace didn't need to ask who.

Version 04.

The dark Grace.

The one who had stepped from a mirror and tried to unravel her mind like a badly written thesis.

"She was sealed," Grace said, frowning.

Ethel nodded grimly. "Yes. And the seal is still there. But someone's... knocking from the inside."

***

Reactivation Request

The council had received a *form*.

Of course they had.

UNIDENTIFIED BUREAU ENTITY REQUESTING REACTIVATION OF VERSION 04

Reason: "For continuity repair"
Emotional Risk Level: Red
Attachment Detected: L117 (Leo)

Do you authorise opening containment cell?
YES / NO

The form had no return address.

Leo studied it.

"That handwriting. It's Watcher script. Old."

Grace swallowed. "But why reactivate her?"

Ethel said, "Because someone out there still believes she's the *real* you."

***

The Goodbye Letter

Before they could respond to the request, a pigeon—different from before, fatter and wearing a top hat—landed on the table.

It dropped a sealed envelope and dramatically keeled over.

Leo sniffed it. "Drama bird."

Grace unfolded the letter.

The handwriting was sharp, fluid, and unmistakably feline.

TO: GRACE
FROM: LILI

I have requested to be erased.
Not because I regret knowing you—
But because too many versions of us exist now,
And I was the one most likely to fracture the rest.

Tell Leo... he was always the better "me."
Tell the fig tree it still owes me five forms and a banana.

And tell the Bureau I never stopped being a cat.
Even when I looked like a man.

Goodnight.

- L

Leo stared at it a long time.

Then said softly, "He really went through with it."

* * *

Echoes and Projections

That night, Leo began *seeing* things.

Not hallucinations.

Not exactly.

When Grace spoke, sometimes her words glowed in the air like subtitles in a language only he knew.

When she remembered something strong—a song, a smell, a feeling—Leo saw the ghost of another version of her shimmer just behind her, like a flicker in a candle.

He asked Ethel.

She said, "Welcome to Watcher-grade emotional projection. You're perceiving version bleed."

He muttered, "No one warned me it'd be this... *loud*."

She shrugged. "You've got a heart full of cats. What did you expect?"

* * *

What Claremont Really Is

Later, Grace was making toast when she asked:

"Leo. Do you think we've... been here before?"

He looked up from the radiator.

"Yes. But not like this."

She sat beside him. "I keep thinking Claremont isn't a place. It's a *state*."

Leo purred softly.

"It's a version trap," he said. "A convergence point. A garden where all the almosts come to bloom."

Grace blinked.

"And we live here?"

He nodded.

"Every day. Choosing to be *this* version. Together."

* * *

Interlude: The Orange Cat's Journal (Entry #42)

04 stirs.
Li Li gone.
Me? Upgraded.

Grace glows sometimes.
I see all her might-have-beens.
She still chooses cereal at midnight.

Maybe that's what makes her real.

Maybe that's what makes *me* real too.

* * *

Part 8

The Teahouse of Reflected Selves

They called it The Teahouse at the Edge of Edits.

To the rest of Claremont, it was just an abandoned café behind the allotments, covered in ivy and pigeon graffiti.

But Leo said it shimmered in Watcher-vision. Not with power—*with possibility*.

Grace stepped through its door, and the bell above the entrance rang in reverse.

Time hiccupped.

Then she was inside.

Wooden chairs. Dusty lace curtains. The scent of bergamot and forgotten apologies.

Version 04 was waiting at a corner table.

She looked like Grace.

Only colder.

Sharper.

Like a version that had survived by cutting everything soft out of herself.

* * *

The Conversation with 04

"You came," said 04, sipping tea that steamed but never cooled.

"You asked," Grace replied.

They sat in silence for a moment, staring at each other like mirrors that resented being looked into.

04 broke first.

"I wasn't evil, you know."

"I know," Grace said softly. "Just unfinished."

04 laughed bitterly. "They locked me up because I wouldn't lie to myself. I *remembered everything*. The tree. The collapse. The cats. All of it."

Grace looked down. "But you didn't *choose* any of it."

04's hand trembled.

"No," she whispered. "I was chosen *for* it. And then blamed for not fitting the script."

* * *

The Offer

A folder materialised on the table.

Stamped with the Bureau's broken seal.

CONDITIONAL PAROLE
Subject: Version 04
Terms: Transfer of primary emotional alignment to G-03
Outcome: Merge / Rewrite
Risk: Identity Complication

"I'm not asking to overwrite you," 04 said. "Just to stop... echoing."

Grace reached out.

Placed her hand over hers.

"Then come home. As memory. Not shadow."

*　*　*

The Merge

They stood.

The teahouse folded inward.

Chairs dissolved.

Curtains sighed.

And Grace felt her chest bloom—no, *stitch*—with a fierce clarity.

I was the Grace who fought.
I was the Grace who stayed.
I am the Grace who remembers both.

Outside, Leo waited.

When she opened the door, he looked up.

"You're heavier," he said.

"Emotionally?"

"No, I meant literally. You're carrying two whole backstories now."

Grace smiled.

"Then carry me."

He grumbled.

Then jumped into her arms anyway.

* * *

Council Resolution

Back at the hall, Ethel read the final vote.

"Version 04 successfully reabsorbed.
Emotional signature stabilised.
Grace Harper reclassified as Class-Three Emotional Convergence Entity.

Suggested category:
Sentient Domestic Reality Anchor."

Leo muttered, "Snappy."

Grace shrugged. "At least I get a category now."

Chair-Councillor Norris cleared his throat.

"There's one last file," he said. "Found in the Loophole Garden. Addressed to both of you. Sealed by... Claremont itself."

* * *

The Final Message

The paper was warm.

Handwritten.

Oddly... feline.

**To Grace and Leo,

You chose presence over perfection.
Companionship over clarity.
Toast over transformation.

That makes you rare.

You've both earned peace.
Until next version.

Signed,
Claremont (Rooted Version)**

Leo read it.

Then said, "Well. I suppose we *are* finally official."

Grace nodded.

And for the first time since the Root Tree cracked, she truly felt real.

* * *

Interlude: The Orange Cat's Journal (Entry #43)

Version 04:
Merged
Not erased

Grace:
One soul, two timelines
Still burns toast

Me:
Still orange
Still here

Still hers

* * *

Part 9

The Watcher Invitation

The official invitation came in the least official way possible: slipped under Grace's front door, written on a napkin from the Claremont Fish Bar.

It read:

TO: G-03 (Grace Harper)

You have been selected for provisional Watcher status
on account of:

- surviving emotional recursion
- filing more than three valid complaints
- making peace with at least one version of yourself

Training to begin... whenever you're ready.
No rush.
(Seriously. We've seen your calendar.)

Yours occasionally,
– W Bureau, Cat-Side Division

Grace turned to Leo.

"Cat-Side Division?"

He rolled over on the windowsill. "It means we're the emotionally volatile ones."

"Oh. Great."

* * *

The Synchronisation Incident

Just as Grace was trying to process *that*, a sudden hum shook the flat.

Not a scary hum.

More like a group of vacuum cleaners attempting to harmonise.

Then—

POP!

Leo split into two.

Literally.

One Leo looked exactly the same.
The other wore a bow tie and had a slight French accent.

"Oh no," Leo muttered.

Bow Tie Leo meowed dramatically. "Enfin! I am free from ze constraints of narrative!"

More pops.

A third Leo appeared. Wearing aviator sunglasses.

A fourth—tiny, kitten-sized—started demanding toast.

* * *

The Multiversal Cat Parade

Claremont streets filled with versions of Leo.

- One was neon green and claimed to be "from the year 2099."
- One recited poetry in Latin.
- One was just a particularly smug-looking pillow with ears.

Council members scrambled to contain the situation.

Ethel ran past shouting, "They're clogging the hedgerows! Someone deploy the catnip spray!"

The twelve-year-old Watcher-in-training floated above the chaos with a clipboard. "This is fine. Probably."

Grace sighed.

Leo (her Leo, she hoped) appeared beside her.

"Okay," he said. "I know what happened."

"Do tell."

* * *

What Happened, In Short

Leo cleared his throat.

"When you merged with Version 04, and I received Watcher-lite powers, our resonance attracted every version of me who was *slightly unregistered*. It's like we threw a dinner party and forgot to tell the other guests to stay home."

"So... you *are* the original?"

He frowned. "Technically, I'm the most *emotionally aligned* one."

"I'll take it."

"Good. Because I'm also the one who knows how to reverse this."

Grace smiled. "Let me guess. We have to file a complaint."

Leo nodded. "You know me so well."

* * *

The Final Complaint

They marched back to the Oversight Hall, dodging two Leos having a rap battle.

Grace slapped a form on the table.

"COMPLAINT: Too many cats.
CAUSE: Interdimensional leakage via emotional convergence.
SOLUTION: Re-sync to default."

Chair-Councillor Norris blinked. "That's the most coherent filing we've had in weeks."

"Does that mean—"

A bell rang.

The projector turned on.

All across Claremont, the extra Leos winked out of existence with tiny meows of theatrical disappointment.

* * *

Back to One Cat

Just like that—Claremont was calm.

The hedges untrampled.

The toast untouched.

And Leo, still orange, still smug, was once again singular.

Grace looked at him.

He blinked back.

Then flopped onto her lap like the world's most casually omniscient pillow.

"Never leave again," she said.

"Too much paperwork," he mumbled.

* * *

Interlude: The Orange Cat's Journal (Entry #44)

Me(s):
– All returned
– Except me
– The one she picked

Grace:
– Watcher, kind of
– Whole, mostly
– Makes tea like a wizard

Claremont:
Still standing
Still strange

We're good.
For now.

Part 10

One Last Letter, and Then Toast

The next morning, Grace opened her letterbox to find a singular envelope.

No stamp.

No address.

Just one paw print in orange ink, and the faint scent of fish fingers.

Inside was a note written in aggressively curly handwriting.

**To: Grace Harper & Co. (especially the feline)

Subject: Status Update & Emotional Clearance**

Your cat registration is now complete.
Your Watcher status is pending.
Your emotional reality alignment has been marked "stable-ish."

We regret to inform you that Claremont remains strange.

Sincerely,
The Department of Mildly Impossible Affairs
(Feline Subdivision)

P.S. The fig tree says hi.
P.P.S. It still lies.

Grace stared at the letter, then folded it neatly and stuck it on the fridge next to a pizza coupon that had expired in 2017.

* * *

A Very Normal Afternoon

Later that day, she and Leo sat in the garden.

The real one.

No floating benches.

No whispering hydrangeas.

Just a lawn, a plastic flamingo, and a breeze that smelled like laundry and possibility.

Grace was reading a book.

Leo was sleeping on her feet.

Occasionally, his ears twitched as though arguing with a dream-version of himself about whether croissants were superior to crumpets.

At one point, a pigeon walked by and winked at them.

Grace didn't even flinch.

*　*　*

Final Reflections

"So," Leo mumbled, not bothering to open his eyes, "are you going to accept the Watcher role?"

Grace tilted her head.

"Maybe. But not today."

"Why not?"

"I like this version of the afternoon," she said. "No forms. No collapsing timelines. Just you. And tea."

Leo purred.

"I approve. Emotionally and grammatically."

She grinned. "Do cats care about grammar?"

He opened one eye.

"We *invented* it."

*　*　*

And Then

Grace leaned back in her chair.

Leo curled into a ball.

The clouds shifted.

A breeze rolled through the hedges.

And from somewhere faint and far, a voice echoed:

"You thought registering a cat was hard?
Wait until you try renewing the licence…"

* * *

Final Interlude: The Orange Cat's Journal (Entry #45)

Registered.
Rooted.
Remembered.

Her reality is mine now.
Mine is hers.

Still orange.
Still feline.

Possibly divine.

Time for toast.

Chapter Seven: The Cat, the Code, and the Council Tax

Part 1

The Bill That Winked

It started with a bill.

Not the kind that ruins your life outright—but the kind that creeps in politely and then refuses to leave.

"Council Tax Adjustment Notice," Grace read aloud, frowning.

Leo, from the radiator, blinked slowly. "Didn't you already pay that?"

"I *did*. Twice. Once with direct debit, once emotionally."

But this wasn't a normal bill. Because this one had a watermark that shimmered when she tilted it—spelling out:

"This is not a bill. This is a message."

Leo jumped down.

"Oh good. I love fiscal espionage."

* * *

Interlude: The Orange Cat's Journal (Entry #46)

Council tax as interdimensional messaging system:
```
- Efficient
- Evil
- Typical
```

Grace still thinks bills are boring.
She's wrong. Some bills purr when you read them backwards.

I remain orange.
I remain mildly concerned.
I also swallowed something I can't explain to the vet.

* * *

Part 2

Hidden Code in the Sofa

Later that evening, Leo pawed something out from under the sofa.

A furball.

But not one of his.

This one pulsed.

Grace stared at it.

Leo tapped it with a claw.

It uncurled.

And projected a message in midair:

Node 7¼ Active
Surveillance compromised
Bureau Resurgence Confirmed

Status: REDACTED
Response: CONSUME TO CONFIRM**

Grace gawked. "They want us to *eat* it?!"

Leo sniffed it, grimaced, and nudged it into a bowl of milk.

"Technically, I'm the one with an expendable stomach. Bottoms up."

He swallowed.

Then burped out a binary code.

Grace reached for her laptop.

* * *

Interlude: The Orange Cat's Journal (Entry #47)

(After Part 2)

Node 7¼:
— Not a shop
— Not a node
— Possibly a haunted toaster disguised as infrastructure

Meowcroft has ears sharper than my claws.
I do not trust cats in suits. They usually work in middle management.

Grace: curious, alert, slightly overcaffeinated.

Me: suspicious, fluffy, armed with emotional data.

***

Part 3

Emotional Forensics and the AI Cat from Hell

Meowcroft gestured, and a chair unfolded from the wall like a bureaucratic orchid.

"L117," he said to Leo, "we're initiating a Class-Three Feline Emotional Audit.
You've been radiating *unsanctioned narrative influence*."

Leo jumped onto the chair with the air of someone who had already written his own defence.

Grace leaned in. "You okay with this?"

Leo gave her a sideways look. "Please. I once debated a ghost over the ethical implications of tuna. I'm built for this."

A strange click echoed.

From the shadows emerged a silver-furred cat with glowing blue eyes.

It blinked once and said, in a voice like a phone menu,

"I am AuditorCat v2.4. Prepared to analyse emotional leakage."

Leo stood.

"This is going to get ugly."

* * *

The Emotional Stand-Off

AuditorCat extended its claws.

Digital projections hovered in the air—charts, colour-coded data points, a suspicious number of pie graphs.

"You have exceeded your daily quota of:
– Emotional Sentimentality (4.8x)
– Loyalty Persistence (6.1x)
– Unauthorised Affection (9.3x)"

Leo scoffed. "I'm a cat. Affection is already anomalous."

"You initiated 2.7 purrs per hour for 36 hours straight."

"I was buffering," Leo retorted.

AuditorCat hissed. "You *nuzzled*."

Grace gasped. "Leo, how could you."

Leo growled. "I was vulnerable! It was raining! She made toast!"

* * *

Glasses of Deep Perception

While the cats squared off, Meowcroft handed Grace a case.

Inside: glasses.

Not normal ones. They shimmered at the edges and hummed faintly.

"These will let you see what has not yet been emotionally recorded," he said. "Feelings unregistered by bureaucracy. Real ones."

She put them on.

And gasped.

The room around her filled with shimmering trails:

- Regret lingering in Meowcroft's tail flicks.
- Frustration simmering under Leo's fur.
- And—deep beneath the glowing coldness—AuditorCat's echo of *longing*.

Grace whispered, "They're all pretending."

Meowcroft nodded.

"As do all bureaucrats, eventually."

* * *

The Verdict

The graphs stopped.

AuditorCat narrowed its eyes.

Leo licked a paw dramatically.

Then a bell dinged.

"Audit complete. Subject L117:

Status: Emotionally overloaded
Cause: Improper bonding with Primary Human

Recommendation:
– Demotion: REJECTED
– Praise: GRUDGINGLY APPROVED"

A tiny medal floated down from the ceiling.

It read:

"FELINE: Emotionally Compromised but Technically Functional."

Leo batted it aside. "I'll eat it later."

Grace gave him a look.

He sighed. "Fine. I'll frame it."

* * *

Interlude: The Orange Cat's Journal (Entry #48)

AuditorCat:
– Sharp
– Cold
– Lonely

I think it misses being touched.
I didn't purr at it, but I thought about it. That counts.

Grace saw it all. With glasses that see unclaimed feelings.

She didn't say anything.
She just smiled.

That's why I chose her.
Even when I didn't have to.

* * *

Part 4

Faye and the Fog of Forgotten Feelings

Claremont looked the same.

Until Grace put on the Bureau glasses again.

Then everything shimmered.

Not visually—but emotionally.

A neighbour's smile now came with a ghost-trail of buried exhaustion.
A passing dog left behind anxiety like a cold sneeze.
Even the bin outside her flat seemed to emit faint embarrassment (probably because someone had thrown away an entire unpeeled pineapple).

"Okay," Grace whispered. "This is too much."

Leo, perched on her shoulder like a smug parrot, meowed softly. "Welcome to my world."

* * *

The Girl Who Remembers Feelings

They found Faye—the weirdly observant 9-year-old from next door—sitting on the pavement, drawing something on the concrete with a stick of chalk and a sense of cosmic purpose.

Grace crouched. "What are you drawing?"

Faye looked up, eyes glowing faintly behind oversized glasses of her own.

"A map of what people don't say."

Leo blinked. "She's *one of them*."

Grace whispered, "One of what?"

Faye smiled. "I'm a Keeper. I keep the feelings you throw away."

She pointed to a shape in her chalk.

It looked like Leo.
But smaller.
And orange.

* * *

The Unspoken Sentence

Faye tapped the drawing with her stick.

"This one is yours," she said to Leo. "From when you were still orange. You left something unsaid."

Leo stepped forward slowly.

Faye stood, pulled a marble from her pocket, and handed it to him.

"It's in here."

Leo stared at the tiny glass sphere.

Inside: swirling orange mist. A whisper trapped in light.

He touched it with one claw.

And the words echoed.

"You were the home I never expected to survive in."

Grace gasped.

Faye grinned. "Now it's yours again."

* * *

Echo Integration

Leo didn't speak.

He just climbed onto Grace's lap, head pressed to her heart, and let the echo settle into place.

No Bureau forms.

No fig trees.

Just a moment of truth, released and accepted.

Grace whispered, "How long did that sit inside you?"

Leo answered, very quietly, "Since the night he left."

Faye saluted them both with her chalk and skipped away.

Her map remained behind, shimmering slightly.

***

Interlude: The Orange Cat's Journal (Entry #49)

Faye:
– Not Bureau
– Not Watcher
– Just... honest

She kept my last words.
Not because she had to.
But because someone should.

Grace knows now.

I'm more than memory.

I'm continuity.

I am orange. And I am staying.

***

Part 5

The Brick That Spoke in Regret

Grace wandered down Claremont High Street, Leo curled across her shoulders like a fashionable but morally ambiguous scarf.

She wore the Bureau glasses again.

And immediately regretted it.

The emotional noise of Claremont hit like a soggy dishcloth of unresolved tension.

Every mailbox radiated mild betrayal.
Every shopfront held echoes of unpurchased dreams.

The Pret-a-Manger had the lingering scent of rushed breakups and lukewarm oat milk.

Leo whispered, "We're walking through the emotional bin of a small town."

Grace nodded. "And it *reeks* of repressed ambition."

* * *

The Emotional Janitor

Outside the closed-down video rental (which was *still* somehow receiving new stock), an old man swept the pavement with unnecessary aggression.

He wore a raincoat, fingerless gloves, and the expression of someone who had once cleaned up after a supernatural tantrum and never quite recovered.

"Ah, you see it now too," he grunted, without looking up.

Grace stopped. "Excuse me?"

The man jabbed his broom at her. "Glasses. You've got 'em. Means they gave you the code. Bureau lackey or rogue empath?"

"Neither?"

He chuckled. "Same difference."

Leo whispered, "Careful. He's ex-Cleaner."

Grace raised an eyebrow. "Cleaner?"

The man grinned. "Emotional remediation, luv. We used to scrub down entire towns after breakups and bad decisions."

He pointed at the pavement.

"Some regrets stain deeper than blood."

* * *

The Speaking Brick

He stepped aside and gestured at the ground.

One brick, slightly darker than the others, pulsed faintly.

Grace knelt.

The brick whispered.

"You almost stayed.
You almost said yes.
You almost became a version of yourself that believed in someone again."

She blinked.

Leo leaned in. "Oh wow. That's... disturbingly specific."

The old man nodded. "Bricks keep what your walls won't."

Grace stood.

"So this isn't about cats anymore, is it?"

He snorted. "It never was. You're not registering a pet. You're registering *permission to belong again*."

* * *

A Brick in the Bag

Grace pulled the brick free.

It was heavier than expected.

Warm.

Leo whispered, "Put it in the tote. Emotional infrastructure is fashionable now."

She dropped it in with a thud.

The street sighed.

A few of the louder regrets faded to background static.

The old man lit a cigarette with a Bureau-issued match.

"Keep collecting them," he said. "The bits of you you didn't know you needed."

Then he vanished into the alley behind the nail salon.

* * *

Interlude: The Orange Cat's Journal (Entry #50)

Claremont:
– Haunted
– Honest
– Full of forgotten maybes

Grace now carries one. A brick made of an "almost."
I think she'll collect more.

Me? I already belong.

She gave me that the day she opened her door.

No registration required.

Just toast.

* * *

Part 6

The Regret Bus and the Cat That Came Before

The letter came folded into a fortune cookie.

Grace cracked it open and read the note inside:

Summons:
You have been selected for the Claremont Regret Archival Pilot Programme™.
Please bring all portable fragments of unresolved emotional infrastructure.
Wear comfortable shoes.

Departure in 18 minutes.
– Emotional Waste Management Unit (Subsection B: Personal Baggage)**

Leo squinted at it.

"We're going on a *regret bus?*"

Grace glanced at the brick in her tote.

She nodded.

"I guess we are."

* * *

The Bus That Doesn't Exist on Wednesdays

At exactly 3:33 PM, a yellow-and-teal double-decker emerged from a fog that smelled like overdue library books.

Its destination board read:

Route 0: Almosts, If-Onlys, and Would-Have-Beens

The driver was a fox in a waistcoat who accepted emotional currency only.

Grace paid with a dried daisy from her coat pocket and one heartfelt sigh.

Leo offered a lint ball from 2019 and the memory of a purr he once held back.

Accepted.

They boarded.

The seats were warm and oddly forgiving.

Outside, the world blinked.

* * *

The Cat Before Leo

In the back of the bus sat a cat.

Not just any cat.

Grey.

Short-furred.

And unmistakably familiar.

Grace froze.

Leo's fur puffed ever so slightly.

The grey cat opened one eye.

"You finally replaced me."

Leo hissed. "You're dead."

The cat purred. "Emotionally, sure. Bureau-dead? Not quite."

Grace whispered, "Is that... Momo?"

Momo rolled over lazily. "I'm the residual projection of Momo. The unresolved competition. The cat that left first."

Leo's ears twitched.

"You were barely housebroken."

Momo grinned. "And yet she still cried more when I left than when you arrived."

* * *

Confrontation on the Regret Route

The bus swayed gently.

Everyone else was quiet—watching two emotional spectres do emotional karate.

Grace stood.

"Stop it," she said.

Momo and Leo paused.

"You were both real," she said. "In your own ways. In your own versions of me."

Momo blinked.

Leo looked away.

Grace pulled the brick from her bag and placed it on the seat between them.

"I carried this for both of you."

The bus driver gave a satisfied nod.

Somewhere, a bell dinged softly.

Momo's form shimmered.

Then smiled.

"Good.
That means I can rest."

He vanished like a sigh.

*　*　*

Interlude: The Orange Cat's Journal (Entry #51)

Momo.
Older. Grayer. Quieter.
Still had claws.

She left first. I stayed second.

But we both mattered.

Grace chose me.
But she mourned her.

I don't need to be the only one.
Just the one that stayed.

* * *

Part 7

The Recycling Centre for Unshed Tears

The Regret Bus rolled to a halt outside a building that looked like a cross between a brutalist cathedral and a laundromat. A flickering sign read:

Claremont Emotional Waste Management Facility – Subsection B: Things Left Unsaid
By Appointment or Emotional Emergency Only

Grace and Leo stepped off the bus. The air smelled like lavender, rain, and old letters never sent.

A receptionist-slash-oracle waved them in with a clipboard shaped like a broken heart.

"This way. You're here to drop off a persistent fragment."

Grace blinked. "The brick?"

Leo added, "Or possibly me."

* * *

Sorting by Emotional Density

They were led down a corridor lined with conveyor belts.

On them: memories.

- A melted ice cream cone handed to the wrong child.
- A voicemail deleted before it was listened to.
- A wedding invitation never mailed.
- A friendship bracelet stretched out of shape.

Grace placed her brick on the belt.

It was gently carried away, humming a soft tune that sounded suspiciously like a lost lullaby.

Leo looked around.

"So… this is where feelings go to not haunt you?"

The oracle nodded. "Or to find new forms. Regret is just an emotion waiting for a better job title."

* * *

The Transfer of Temporary Authority

As the brick vanished into the glowing bin of 'Handled At Last', Leo's tail glowed briefly.

A scroll popped into existence with a tiny puff of glitter.

NOTICE OF INTERIM GUARDIANSHIP

Feline Entity L117 is hereby granted:
– Temporary Emotional Proxy Access (Human: G-03)
– Limited Intervention Rights (up to 3 nudges per day)
– Full Toast Allocation Authority

Leo purred. "I outrank most small deities now."

Grace rolled her eyes. "So basically, you're my emotional cat-sitter."

"Guardian," he corrected smugly.

* * *

The Room of Forked Paths

They were led next into a chamber with twelve doors.

Each was labelled with a sentence Grace had never said aloud:

- "I forgive you."
- "I need help."
- "I loved you too."
- "Please don't go."

Leo touched one door and winced.

"They all hum."

Grace frowned. "Which one do I open?"

The oracle shrugged. "Only you can decide what version of yourself you want to become.
Just know—any door you don't open today, you'll meet again in a different form."

* * *

She Chose "Please don't go."

It opened with a sigh.

Inside: a park bench, a warm breeze, and her mother's coat still smelling like old perfume.

No one else was there.

Just the echo of a moment never voiced.

Grace sat down.

Said the words.

Felt nothing happen.

Then everything.

Leo pressed against her leg.

No magic.
No Bureau badge.
Just breath.

And something inside her stopped waiting.

* * *

Interlude: The Orange Cat's Journal (Entry #52)

Door chosen:
"Please don't go."

She said it too late.
But also:
Just in time.

Grief isn't a door.
It's a hallway.

But even halls need somewhere to start.

I watched her sit.
I didn't speak.

Some things you hold by being quiet near them.

* * *

Part 8

The Town That Forgot What It Felt

When Grace and Leo returned to Claremont, something was off.

Very off.

Mrs. Jeffries from No. 6 was weeping into her begonias while loudly declaring, "I'm *so proud* of this soil!"

A man outside the newsagent was throwing confetti at traffic lights, insisting he was *furious* with the government.

A teenage couple was breaking up while giggling hysterically.

Grace whispered, "What... happened?"

Leo sniffed the air.

"Reality leak. One of the doors you *didn't* open must've seeped through."

Grace groaned. "Is that allowed?"

He shrugged. "It's Claremont. Emotional reality is a guideline at best."

* * *

Misfiled Feelings Everywhere

They passed a woman slapping her own mailbox, muttering, "I'm just *too happy* to deal with this nonsense!"

The postman was delivering letters in a top hat while sobbing softly.

Grace said, "Okay. This is dangerously British."

Leo agreed. "Repressed chaos with biscuits. We need to re-stabilise perception."

"How?"

He pointed to the "Interim Guardian" scroll still floating next to his tail.

"I get three nudges. I'm using one. On you."

"On me?!"

He sat.

Tail wrapped neatly.

"You're about to make the wrong decision for the right reasons."

✳ ✳ ✳

The Wrong Decision

Grace was walking toward the community centre.

Inside: Meowcroft.

Waiting.

He'd invited her to formally join the Bureau's *Observer Corps*.

A desk.
A badge.
A folder of decisions not yet made.

She was about to say yes.

Because she was flattered.

Because it sounded important.

Because maybe finally, she'd belong somewhere.

But Leo stepped in front of her.

And looked up.

"No."

She blinked. "No?"

"You're accepting because you *think* this is what people like you do. Not because it's what *you* want."

* * *

Grace Steps Back

She stared at him.

Then at the door.

Then at her reflection in the Bureau glasses.

She didn't look ready.

She looked... rehearsed.

Grace slowly stepped back.

Leo nodded.

"One nudge left," he said. "Two if I purr extra loudly."

The town around them still buzzed with mismatched feelings.

But Grace?

She felt aligned again.

* * *

Interlude: The Orange Cat's Journal (Entry #53)

Misfiled emotions.
Laughter when you mean pain.
Rage when you mean fear.
Love when you mean nothing yet.

Grace nearly said yes to being someone else's version of herself.

I stopped her.

She thinks I saved her.

But truth is:
I remembered who she really was before she forgot.

That's what guardians do.
Even orange ones.

* * *

Part 9

A Town Re-labelled

Grace and Leo stood at the centre of Claremont.

Leo balanced on a bench like a judgmental librarian. Grace held a notepad and the glasses that revealed emotion for what it really was.

Their mission: relabel everything.

Correctly.

"You ready?" Leo asked.

"No," Grace said. "But I've got the pen."

They started with the florist.

She'd been shouting at roses.

Grace tapped the counter.

"Your real feeling is grief."

The woman blinked.

Then cried.

Then made tea.

* * *

Operation: Emotional Truth Bomb

Next: the corner shop.

A boy throwing jam jars.

Labelled: "Anger."

Grace rewrote it: "Loneliness."

The jam-throwing stopped.

Then the busker outside the pub—singing sarcastic breakup songs.

Leo sniffed.

"Shame," he diagnosed.

Grace relabelled it: "Hope. Unexpressed."

The busker played something soft and unguarded.

Coins poured in.

"People," Leo muttered, "are very bad at their own feelings."

Grace smiled. "That's why they have cats."

* * *

The Source of the Chaos

They followed the strongest emotional static to the Claremont Post Office.

Long closed.

Always humming.

Inside, a single undelivered letter floated mid-air, spinning slowly, glowing faintly.

Grace reached for it.

Leo hissed. "Careful."

She opened the envelope.

Inside: a confession.

**To R—
I never told you. I loved you from the beginning.
I lied about the flat. I stayed for you.
I left because I thought I wasn't enough.
I was wrong.

– G**

Leo sniffed. "Unfiled love. Most volatile type."

* * *

Filing the Unspoken

Grace folded the letter.

Lit a single candle.

And said, gently, "Delivered."

A soft *ping* filled the room.

The town sighed.

Emotions settled.

People stopped yelling at bins.

*　*　*

Interlude: The Orange Cat's Journal (Entry #54)

Emotions don't go away.
They wait.

Sometimes in letters.
Sometimes in songs.
Sometimes in toast crusts you didn't eat.

Grace didn't run this time.
She named what hurt.

That's magic.
Bureau didn't invent it.

We did.

You.
Me.
All the orange cats in all the possible kitchens.

***

Part 10

Renewal Application Pending

Two days after the chaos settled, Grace received a letter.

The envelope was Bureau-grey, sealed with a wax stamp of a yawning cat.

Inside: one form.

Blank.

Title:

CAT CERTIFICATE – RENEWAL APPLICATION

(Terms may vary according to emotional realities, lunar positioning, and toast availability.)

No instructions.
No boxes.
Just a single line at the bottom:

"You may now add a second."

***

Conversations on the Windowsill

Grace held the letter up.

"Leo."

He looked up from the radiator. "Mmhmm?"

"They want me to register… another."

He blinked.

"Cat or concept?"

Grace frowned. "They don't say."

Leo stretched, tail curling like punctuation. "You're not required to accept."

"But if I do?"

He hopped onto the windowsill.

"You invite something new. A risk. A choice. Another version of love."

She stared at the blank page.

Then smiled.

"Maybe. But only if we keep the orange one."

Leo purred. "Wise woman."

* * *

The Toast Returns

That night, Grace made toast.

Proper toast.

With real butter, not whatever substitute the fridge had been guilting her into using.

She split the last piece in half.

Set one on the plate.

Dropped the other on the floor, just the way Leo liked it—slightly tragic, with the butter side down.

He didn't eat it immediately.

Instead, he rested a paw on it.

And whispered, "Application accepted."

* * *

Final Interlude: The Orange Cat's Journal (Entry #55)

Renewal begins with silence.

You don't add love because you're missing something.
You add love because there's space.

The form is blank.
The decision isn't.

We've filed all the feelings.
We've forgiven the mail.

I am the first cat.

I won't be the last.

Chapter Eight: Two Cats, One Toast Crisis

Part 1

The Booted Intruder

Opening Scene:
Grace wakes to find her toast missing. Again.
Only this time, there's a handwritten note:
"Tried to wait. Smelled too good. Will make up for it.
— O"

Leo sits at the foot of the bed.

Silent.

Judging.

Grace: "...there's another cat in this flat, isn't there?"
Leo (without blinking): "She wears boots indoors. Nothing is sacred."

Door creaks open.

A poised black-and-white feline enters with the quiet dignity of a diplomat in a hat shop.

Olive: "I hope you like your marmalade smug."

* * *

Part 2

Olive, Officially Rude

Leo stared at Olive.

Olive stared back.

Their shared silence could have curdled oat milk.

Grace sat between them at the kitchen table, trying to look like a neutral Scandinavian design element.

"So," she said, spreading jam with unconvincing cheer, "do either of you want toast?"

Leo: "You know the answer."

Olive: "If it's not sourdough, I'd rather chew bureaucracy."

Grace blinked. "Okay then. Toast for me."

Leo narrowed his eyes. "She stole mine."

"I left a note," Olive purred, sipping oat milk like it was a political statement. "The ethical implications are therefore null."

* * *

The Registration Office Returns

Grace took both cats—reluctantly, on separate sides of a single large tote bag—to the Claremont Pet Registration Office.

"Back again," said the receptionist, who was either a man or a cactus in a tie.

"This time," Grace explained, "it's a two-cat situation."

He handed her a form that smelled of vinegar and compromise.

Form 220-B: Dual Feline Emotional Residency Declaration
Note: Secondary cat cannot be registered without existing cat's nonverbal approval.

Leo made a sound that could only be described as a passive-aggressive sigh.

Olive licked her paw.

"Do I need to curtsey?" she asked sweetly.

Leo flicked his tail.

"You need to stop performing intelligence like it's a competition."

* * *

What the Forms Reveal

While Grace filled in the details, the system printed a "Compatibility Report" between Leo and Olive.

It read:

Emotional History Detected:
- Previous cohabitation detected (Cycle: 5.2.9β)
- Role Conflict: Emotional Anchor vs Emotional Assessor
- Incident Noted: "Toast Event (Unacknowledged)"

Grace raised an eyebrow. "What's the Toast Event?"

Both cats turned simultaneously.

"We. Don't. Discuss. That."

* * *

Tension in the Flat

Back home, the emotional atmosphere thickened like undercooked porridge.

Grace attempted peace by introducing "designated windowsill shifts."

Leo took the left, Olive the right.

Neither was satisfied.

Then came the worst betrayal.

At 2:47 PM, Leo returned to find Olive sleeping in *his* sun patch.

Not the general sun patch.

His.

She opened one eye.

"Time is a social construct."

He hissed. "And so is your right to breathe near me."

* * *

Interlude: The Orange Cat's Journal (Entry #56)

Olive wears logic like a bowtie.
Always symmetrical. Always smug.

We shared a mission once. A kitchen. A couch.
Then toast happened.

I forgave her.
Just not with words. Or feelings.

Now we're registered together.
I don't know if I'm furious or home.

Grace is happy.

So I'll allow it.

For now.

* * *

Part 3

The Emotional Filing Cabinet That Purrs

That evening, Grace tried to unwind on the sofa with a cup of chamomile tea and a quiz show hosted by a man who looked suspiciously like a sentient gherkin.

Leo sat on the armrest, radiating disapproval.

Olive sprawled across the throw blanket like she owned the mortgage.

Then it happened.

Grace sighed. The kind of sigh with layers.

Olive stirred. Ears twitching.

"Frustration," she announced.

Leo snapped, "It was clearly resignation."

"Incorrect. Upper-chest tension. Eyebrow dip. Emotional code F1–Gamma. Frustration."

Grace blinked. "What—how do you know that?"

"I trained in the Swiss Alps with an archive full of repressed librarians," Olive replied.

Leo hissed. "You say that about everything."

* * *

Emotional Accuracy vs Emotional Loyalty

"Let me guess," Olive continued, twitching her tail. "You feel like you're not doing *enough* even when you're doing *too much*. You think feeling tired is a failure of character. And you're still blaming yourself for burning that almond croissant last Tuesday."

Grace's jaw dropped.

Leo tried to speak.

"Actually, she—"

Olive flicked her paw. "Stay in your lane, Orange."

"She was going to cry!"

"She was going to *breathe*. You panic every time she exhales too deeply."

"I'm guarding her emotional bandwidth!"

"You're clogging it with over-filtered concern!"

Grace held up a hand. "Enough."

The cats froze.

She took a sip of tea.

"I hate when you're both right."

* * *

Toast Allocation Dispute #2

The next morning, Grace prepared two pieces of toast.

She placed one on each small plate—labelled in biro: **Leo** and **Olive**.

She turned her back for thirty seconds.

When she returned, Leo had eaten his.

Olive's was untouched.

Except her butter was missing.

Grace turned slowly.

Leo looked... smug.

Too smug.

"You licked her toast," she said flatly.

Leo shrugged. "I was emotionally hungry."

Olive narrowed her eyes.

"That was Category B-Emotional Compensation. *Unauthorised.*"

* * *

The Bureau Notices

A scroll appeared midair.

WARNING: Feline Guardian L117
Violation of Emotional Neutrality Clause
Strike One: Misassigned Appetite

Leo groaned. "They're *always* watching."

Olive licked her paw.

"Strike two is automatic if he drinks my oat milk again."

* * *

Interlude: The Orange Cat's Journal (Entry #57)

I used to be the only one who knew her sighs.

Now Olive knows too.

She doesn't purr.
She pronounces.

But she sees what I miss.

Maybe guardians come in pairs.

Maybe being first doesn't mean being everything.

Still. I miss when the toast had only one plate.

* * *

Part 4

The Trust Tunnel and the Emotional Enrichment Cat Gym

The Claremont Community Centre had recently opened a very niche facility:

The Emotionally Enriched Pet Playground

"For cats with complicated pasts and owners with more feelings than fridge space."

Grace signed the waiver without blinking.

Leo hissed at the "no toast inside the gym" rule.

Olive adjusted her metaphorical monocle.

"Let's do this."

* * *

Obstacle One: The Tunnel of Trust

The first obstacle was a long, enclosed tunnel. Soft walls. No visibility. Emotional echo amplification inside.

"Most cats," said the handler, "get nervous when left alone in their thoughts."

Leo grunted. "Sounds like therapy with carpets."

Olive went first.

Midway, she paused.

Her thoughts echoed:

"Not good enough. Not soft enough. Always second."

She emerged blinking.

Leo followed.

His tunnel echoed:

"She'll choose someone else. I won't matter once there are more. I'm replaceable."

He tripped over the exit.

Grace waited on the other side.

"I heard nothing," she lied.

Both cats knew she hadn't.

But they let it be.

* * *

Obstacle Two: The Climb of Shared Perspective

A pair climb.

Two cats.

One unstable platform.

They had to reach the top together.

Leo scrambled halfway.

Olive sighed. "You're putting all your weight on the left!"

"That's where *your* smugness lives!"

They argued.

The platform tilted.

Grace, sipping her water, muttered, "This is literally every group project I've ever done."

Eventually, Leo let Olive go first.

Then followed.

They made it.

Together.

No toast at the top.

But mutual grumbling was served.

* * *

Trigger Warning: Foam Ball Pit of Suppressed Childhood Memories

Final obstacle.

A pit filled with pastel foam cubes and seemingly innocent music.

Grace stepped in to retrieve her cats.

And froze.

A smell—plastic and dust.

A song—an ice cream truck jingle.

A memory—her mother dropping her off at a birthday party, smiling too brightly, never coming back that day.

She sat in the pit.

Silent.

Eyes unfocused.

* * *

The Cats React

Leo froze.

Olive tilted her head.

"She's relapsing into pre-verbal abandonment anxiety."

Leo hissed. "She's sad."

Olive turned to him.

"This is your intervention."

Leo climbed into the pit.

Curled against Grace's side.

Whispered: "I'm here."

She blinked.

Breathed.

Smiled.

Tears came.

Not loud. Not scary.

Real.

Grace reached over.

Pulled Olive in.

Now they were all in the pit.

Covered in foam.

Emotionally correct.

* * *

Interlude: The Orange Cat's Journal (Entry #58)

Sometimes your human breaks a little.
Not because she's weak.
But because the past doesn't know what time it is.

Olive saw the pattern.
I saw the pain.

We both reached.

That's the job.
Not to fix her.

Just to sit with the version of her that needs holding.

And maybe steal a corner of her sandwich afterwards.
For morale.

* * *

Part 5

The Letter From Later

That night, Grace slept like someone who had emotionally sweat out six years of tension in a foam pit.

Leo and Olive curled at opposite ends of the bed like rival philosophers forced to share a single dissertation.

At 3:13 AM, a scroll materialised in the air. It glittered faintly. Its seal bore a familiar symbol:

A half-eaten sandwich and the phrase:
"Reminder: You're further than you think."

Leo opened it with a claw.

Olive read silently.

To Me – From Me (Later)

You will doubt again.
You will think two cats are too many.
That love divided is love diluted.
But listen:

Two cats will save you.
In ways one never could.

Don't forget to let them fight a little.
It's how they show they're trying.

Also: don't microwave leftover toast. You *always* regret that.

* * *

The Ethics of Disclosure

Leo paced the windowsill.

"She's not ready."

Olive yawned. "That's not your call."

"She *needs* to figure it out on her own."

Olive raised a paw. "It's a letter from her future self. It's literally *already figured out.*"

Leo glared. "You think emotional honesty is a blanket solution."

"I think hiding truth is just slow-motion sabotage."

They stared at each other.

The scroll hovered between them.

Grace snored, oblivious.

Somewhere downstairs, the fridge made a noise of existential uncertainty.

* * *

The Kitchen Duel

By 4:00 AM, the scroll had been moved to the kitchen counter.

So had both cats.

So had three slices of toast, one of which was *mysteriously* missing its crust.

Leo growled. "You think telling her everything is noble. It's lazy."

Olive swiped the air. "You're protecting her, or your *role*?"

Leo paused.

That landed.

They both sat in silence.

Then Olive said, "Let's hide it in the place she always forgets to check."

Leo blinked. "The cutlery drawer?"

"No. The bottom of her to-do list."

They both nodded.

It was the first agreement they'd had since 2019.

* * *

Interlude: The Orange Cat's Journal (Entry #59)

Love is loud.
But also sneaky.

You can care by shouting.
You can care by hiding breakfast scrolls.

Olive and I both want her to be okay.

We just disagree on the packaging.

Someday, she'll read that letter.

And she'll remember this night not by what she knew...

...but by how warm the room felt.

* * *

Part 5

The Letter From Later

That night, Grace slept like someone who had emotionally sweat out six years of tension in a foam pit.

Leo and Olive curled at opposite ends of the bed like rival philosophers forced to share a single dissertation.

At 3:13 AM, a scroll materialised in the air. It glittered faintly. Its seal bore a familiar symbol:

A half-eaten sandwich and the phrase:
"Reminder: You're further than you think."

Leo opened it with a claw.

Olive read silently.

To Me – From Me (Later)

You will doubt again.
You will think two cats are too many.
That love divided is love diluted.
But listen:

Two cats will save you.
In ways one never could.

Don't forget to let them fight a little.
It's how they show they're trying.

Also: don't microwave leftover toast. You *always* regret that.

* * *

The Ethics of Disclosure

Leo paced the windowsill.

"She's not ready."

Olive yawned. "That's not your call."

"She *needs* to figure it out on her own."

Olive raised a paw. "It's a letter from her future self. It's literally *already figured out.*"

Leo glared. "You think emotional honesty is a blanket solution."

"I think hiding truth is just slow-motion sabotage."

They stared at each other.

The scroll hovered between them.

Grace snored, oblivious.

Somewhere downstairs, the fridge made a noise of existential uncertainty.

* * *

The Kitchen Duel

By 4:00 AM, the scroll had been moved to the kitchen counter.

So had both cats.

So had three slices of toast, one of which was *mysteriously* missing its crust.

Leo growled. "You think telling her everything is noble. It's lazy."

Olive swiped the air. "You're protecting her, or your *role*?"

Leo paused.

That landed.

They both sat in silence.

Then Olive said, "Let's hide it in the place she always forgets to check."

Leo blinked. "The cutlery drawer?"

"No. The bottom of her to-do list."

They both nodded.

It was the first agreement they'd had since 2019.

* * *

Interlude: The Orange Cat's Journal (Entry #59)

Love is loud.
But also sneaky.

You can care by shouting.
You can care by hiding breakfast scrolls.

Olive and I both want her to be okay.

We just disagree on the packaging.

Someday, she'll read that letter.

And she'll remember this night not by what she knew...

...but by how warm the room felt.

* * *

Part 6

The Third Cat That Wasn't There (Yet)

Grace stood at the breakfast table, buttering toast in a manner best described as "philosophically distracted."

Leo sniffed the air.

Something was off.

Not the toast.

Grace.

She took a bite, then casually said:

"Do you think three cats is too many?"

The silence that followed was dense enough to host a TED Talk.

Leo's tail twitched like an exposed electrical wire.

Olive, mid-lap of oat milk, froze.

"You're joking," Leo said flatly.

"I'm *just wondering*," Grace replied, buttering too close to the crust. "There's this little tabby at the shelter…"

Leo stared. "What about me?"

Grace blinked. "What *about* you?"

Olive whispered, "Oh dear."

* * *

Emergency Toast Council

An emergency toast council was convened.

Two chairs.

Two plates.

Two cats.

One very crumpled napkin with the title:

"Terms of Multi-Feline Household Governance"

Leo drew a line down the centre.

"I require exclusive rights to the radiator, the east-facing window, and post-8PM lap access."

Olive added: "Fine. I claim emotional diagnostics, post-bathroom door sentry, and veto over human dates."

Leo squinted. "You *never* go to the window."

"I like knowing I could."

They stared.

Then Grace brought in a third plate.

Empty.

* * *

Olive's Slip

Halfway through negotiations, Olive muttered something.

"...not since Marina."

Leo's ears twitched. "What did you say?"

Grace looked up. "Marina?"

Olive froze.

Then very deliberately unfolded her napkin.

Wrote:

"No third parties may be referenced without both cats' consent."

Leo growled. "You said her name."

Olive sighed. "She was... someone we co-guarded."

Grace blinked. "You shared a human?"

Olive nodded.

Leo didn't.

Grace opened her mouth.

Then closed it.

Then said, very quietly:

"Did it end badly?"

Leo said nothing.

Olive looked away.

"Toast burned. That's all."

* * *

Interlude: The Orange Cat's Journal (Entry #60)

Marina.

One kettle.
Two cats.
Three heartbeats out of sync.

We tried.

Olive mapped. I guarded.

It wasn't enough.

Or maybe it was too much, all at once.

That's why this matters.

Grace is different.

She listens.

And maybe this time...

We'll toast on both sides without burning.

* * *

Part 7

The Recording No One Meant to Play

Grace was cleaning behind the toaster.

(Which, for the record, she had *never* done before—suggesting an emotional undertone.)

Her elbow knocked a loose tile.

A click.

A tiny projector unfolded from the wall like it had been waiting politely for years.

A soft chime played.

Then: a flickering image.

Two cats.

One orange. One black-and-white.

A third figure—a woman in a yellow jumper.

Laughing.

Then not.

***

Memory Transmission: The Last Day of Marina

The video showed:

- Marina dancing to a jazz record.
- Olive sitting on a stack of books, ears alert.
- Leo curled on a windowsill, faking sleep.

Then: a phone call.

Her face fell.

She sat.

No one moved.

Later: her suitcase packed.

Leo at the door, watching her leave.

Olive on the bed, staring at her own tail.

Then black.

End of clip.

Grace turned to them.

Quietly:

"You didn't stop her."

Leo's whiskers drooped.

"She didn't let us."

Olive whispered, "We weren't enough."

Grace sat.

Between them.

Then said:

"That's not how it works."

* * *

Kitchen Floor, 2:14 AM

They stayed there.

No music.

No Bureau.

No toast.

Grace reached for both.

Two hands.

Two cats.

"I don't know what I'm doing," she said. "But I know I *want* both of you here."

Leo leaned in.

Olive curled around her ankle.

The silence was full.

Then the fridge gurgled, as if clearing its emotional throat.

Grace laughed.

"Marina would've hated that noise."

Leo grinned. "She thought appliances were plotting."

Olive added, "She wasn't wrong."

* * *

Interlude: The Orange Cat's Journal (Entry #61)

The past plays when no one asks.

But sometimes the reel ends in the middle.

Marina left.
That's true.

But so did we.
We closed the chapter without asking if there were more pages.

Grace saw the clip.
She didn't flinch.

She stayed.

And in staying, she told the past:
"You are not my script."

* * *

Part 8

The Form, the Statement, and the Secret Manuscript

At precisely 9:06 AM, Grace clicked "Submit" on the **Dual Emotional Cat Residency Form**.

It took fifteen seconds for the system to respond.

Application Received

Processing time:
1–3 working emotional cycles

Please prepare a personal statement:
"Why I Choose More Than One."

Grace blinked.

"I didn't prepare an essay," she said.

Leo, from the windowsill: "You *live* the essay."

Olive, from the bookshelf: "You wrote a thesis in toast crumbs last week."

Grace sighed.

Then opened a notepad.

***

Her Statement (Short, Slightly Butter-Stained)

I don't choose because I'm missing something.

I choose because more than one can mean more than enough.

I choose you, Leo. Because you saw the empty room in me before I admitted it existed.

I choose you, Olive. Because you name the storms I pretend are breezes.

And I choose both of you not because I *need* to be guarded—

—but because I want to walk forward with something warm beside me.

Preferably purring. Possibly judging. Absolutely mine.

She hit send.

***

Audit Initiated: Toast Distribution Calibration

That evening, a Bureau drone arrived.

It wore a bowtie and carried a clipboard.

"Toast audit," it said flatly. "Random but emotionally revealing."

The kitchen was inspected.

Crumb trails were measured.

Butter angles assessed.

Leo attempted to bribe it with Earl Grey.

Olive recited legal precedent from a 2007 biscuit case.

Eventually, the drone declared:

"You're operating at 92% toast emotional efficiency. Acceptable. Recommend increase in jam variety."

It left via the laundry chute.

Olive muttered, "Coward."

Leo whispered, "It touched my plate."

* * *

Discovery: The Secret Manuscript

Later that night, Olive found it.

Tucked in Grace's sock drawer, between mismatched wool and a stress ball shaped like David Attenborough.

A notebook.

Handwritten.

Titled:

How to Register a Cat in Another Dimension
By Grace C.

She blinked.

Flipped through.

Stories.

Dialogues.

Toast disputes.

Their toast disputes.

Leo peeked over her shoulder.

"She's writing about us."

Olive smiled.

"For someone who thinks she's uncertain, she's very good at archiving what matters."

Leo whispered, "Should we tell her we know?"

Olive shook her head.

"Not yet. Let her finish the ending first."

* * *

Interlude: The Orange Cat's Journal (Entry #62)

We were never just cats.

We were plot points.
And punchlines.

We are her story.
And she is ours.

I used to worry she'd forget the feelings.

Now I see—
She's writing them down.

That's how you keep love.
Not by holding tighter.
But by telling it in toast, ink, and bedtime fur.

* * *

Part 9

Simulation 8.4B – The Choice Grace Shouldn't See

The Bureau never announces simulations.

They just... begin.

One minute Leo and Olive were in the kitchen, arguing over the ethical parameters of shared teacup rights.

The next—

The walls blurred.

The toast froze mid-air.

Grace vanished.

* * *

The Briefing Room (Made Entirely of Felt)

A Bureau drone appeared.

Name tag: "Daphne"

Personality: Felted disdain.

"Simulation 8.4B. Your human will face a projected future in which one of you is lost.

The scenario is emotionally volatile and completely unnecessary. But highly informative."

Leo hissed. "That's sadistic."

Olive: "That's Bureau standard."

Daphne blinked slowly. "Begin."

* * *

Projected Future Fragment: The Empty Flat

They saw Grace.

Older.

Tired in a specific way.

Her flat was quiet.

Too quiet.

Leo's blanket remained folded in a corner.

Olive's bowl was polished, unused.

She made toast with ritualised sadness.

No one came when the butter fell.

She whispered to the toaster.

Then apologised to it.

Leo turned away.

"I don't want her to see this."

Olive said, "We need to."

* * *

Decision Room: Interfere or Let It Play

Back in the felt room, Daphne waited.

"Would you like to inject context into the simulation?"

Leo: "Yes."

Olive: "No."

They glared at each other.

Then turned to the screen.

Grace was reaching for the window—

Where no cat waited.

Leo spoke first.

"Let's go in. Together."

Olive blinked. Then nodded.

The simulation adjusted.

The toast unfroze.

Grace blinked.

And they appeared.

Leo on the windowsill.

Olive on the table.

Both slightly glowing.

Grace whispered:
"Was I dreaming?"

Leo replied: "Only if we're gone."

* * *

Simulation Ends

Felt walls faded.

Daphne nodded.

"Emotional cohesion: 96%. Above standard. Conditional renewal recommended."

She left without fanfare.

Leo and Olive sat in the echo of the unreal.

Olive said, "We can't protect her from everything."

Leo said, "But we can show her she never has to be alone in it."

* * *

Interlude: The Orange Cat's Journal (Entry #63)

I saw her future.
One of the ones where we weren't there.

She still made toast.
She still waited for purring.

She wasn't broken.
Just... muted.

I hate that sound.

So we came back.

We always will.

Until she forgets how to be sad without smiling.

Until she remembers—two cats is never too many.

*　*　*

Part 10

The Last Page of Toast

The morning light came in at just the right angle.

You know the kind.

The kind that makes everything—
Even the questionable wallpaper—
Look like it belongs in a lifestyle magazine called *Mildly Functional Adults*.

Grace sat at the table.

Her tea was warm.

Her toast, miraculously, unsabotaged.

And her laptop blinked:

Chapter 22: How to Know You're Home
Word count: 67,392

[SUBMIT MANUSCRIPT?]

She hovered. Then clicked.

Somewhere across dimensions, a notification popped up at the Bureau's Department of Literary Overshare.
Someone there cried.

It was beautiful.

* * *

The Contract

That afternoon, a scroll descended.

Golden trim.

Embossed with sardine filigree.

PERMANENT GUARDIANSHIP AGREEMENT

To: Leo (L117) and Olive (O342-P)

You may now choose:

1. Return to the Bureau, elevated rank, no human mess.
2. Stay here. With crumbs. And her.

Decision is binding. Toast is not.

Leo read it first.

Then Olive.

They looked at Grace.

Who said nothing.

Just smiled.

That kind that means:

"I won't ask. But I'll always hope."

Leo signed.

Olive followed.

The scroll disappeared with a satisfying *pop*.

* * *

One Final Disruption

Grace sat that evening on the couch.

Laptop closed.

Book deal pending.

Heart: cautiously full.

Then the doorbell rang.

No one was due.

She opened the door.

Nothing.

Just a small cardboard box.

Inside:

- A cat bed.
- A note:

"Hello. I've heard good things.
I'm not very brave. But I like butter.
– T"

Leo peeked over her shoulder.

Olive sighed.

Grace whispered, "Third?"

Leo groaned.

Olive purred.

Grace smiled.

"Let's make more toast."

* * *

Final Interlude: The Orange Cat's Journal (Entry #64)

Some stories end.

Some just change shape.

We stayed.
She wrote.
The toast ratio improved.

Maybe we'll get a third.
Maybe not.

But this much is true:

Love expands.
Even when it starts with bureaucracy.
Even when it includes someone who bites the butter stick.

Especially then.

This is our file.
Our registration.

May it always stay…
just slightly over the word limit.

Author's Note

If you made it to this page,

you've just read approximately 38,000 words about cats, toast, and the emotional weight of interdimensional paperwork.

You're my kind of person.

This story began as a joke between me and my very smug tabby.

It turned into a way to talk about grief, belonging, and those quiet moments when someone (or some-cat) just sits beside you without asking questions.

Thank you for joining Grace, Leo, and Olive on this slightly magical, slightly bureaucratic journey.

They've made their choice.

They stayed.

And maybe, just maybe, they're ready for the next file.

So am I.

See you in the next chapter.

— Silas B.

A Note to Keke

for the cat who needed no licence to rule my life

Dear Keke,

You never helped me write this book.
You stomped across the keyboard mid-sentence,
closed Word with your tail,
and somehow changed my system language to Russian. Twice.

You had no interest in plot development,
but an obsessive devotion to knocking pens off desks
and scheduling your most violent zoomies during every Zoom call.
You were, by all definitions, the creative saboteur I never fired.

And yet—
when I forgot to scoop your litter box,
you'd pad over, stare me down, and politely poke the box with your paw.
When I made you a tuna birthday cake—complete with a fish-shaped candle—
you were so excited, you launched it off the table like a bottle of champagne.
I laughed for ten minutes.
You didn't.

You believed my work chair was yours,
and on more than one occasion, tried to physically shove me out of it.
You were tiny, but determined.
I moved.

Outside, you were the fierce neighbourhood gremlin—
all scowl and swagger.
But indoors?
A purring heat-seeking missile who demanded cuddles precisely fifteen seconds
after pretending she didn't know me.

You taught me that companionship isn't about obedience,
or behaving on cue.
It's about loyalty, timing, and the sacred art of silent staring.
You were chaos with stripes,
affection wrapped in personal boundaries,
and a reminder that some love arrives on velvet paws
and still takes up the entire room.

This book isn't about you.
But you're in it.
In every moment of strange affection, stubborn connection, and quiet presence.

So thank you—
for supervising my deadlines,

for reminding me who really owned the furniture,
and for being a wildly inconvenient, perfectly unforgettable little soul.

Long may your reign continue.

Yours (never your equal, always your staff),
Silas B.

Printed in Dunstable, United Kingdom

66123410R00231